MR. SEPTEMBER

Calendar Boys Series

NICOLE S. GOODIN

Mr. September
Published by Nicole S. Goodin
ISBN: 978-0-9951276-1-6
Copyright 2019 by Nicole S. Goodin
All rights reserved. ©
First published September 2019

Cover design by Nicole Goodin
Images purchased from Shutterstock
Editing by Spell Bound

For all the babes born in September

CHAPTER ONE

Brody

"Do you think you could stop staring at that blonde chick for maybe... *thirty* seconds so we can finish our conversation?"

Snapped.

"Sorry," I mutter as I reluctantly pull my eyes from the stunning blonde at the bar.

"No, you're not," she grumbles.

"I am." I nudge her hand with mine. "Carry on."

She starts talking again about some woman at her yoga class, and I zone out after a few minutes, my gaze drifting to the blonde in the red dress yet again.

I know I shouldn't be looking when I'm sitting here with Olivia, but I can't help it, it's like a gravitational pull. I can't take my eyes off her for long – not since the moment she walked in.

I glance back at Olivia, and she's still talking, about someone at work this time, and she hasn't noticed that my gaze has drifted once more.

I nod and smile when she does, but I'm not really paying the slightest bit of attention.

The blonde woman is talking to a guy at the bar. I've seen him in here before, hitting on women and, more often than not, taking them home – a different woman every time.

I get a bad vibe from the guy.

I don't know this woman from Eve, but I don't like her talking to that sleaze. It just doesn't sit right with me.

"How's the new job going?" Olivia asks, and I'm forced to focus on her again.

I shrug. "So far, so good. I haven't met the team in person yet, but we've made all of our selections from the pre-season games."

"That's good." She smiles warmly at me, and I feel bad for ignoring her for half of our conversation. "You're going to kill it, B."

I risk one more glance at the blonde, deciding that it will be my last.

She turns away from the bar to look at something over her shoulder, and I see the guy she's talking to move his hand; the movement is so fast I almost don't catch it.

"Did you see that?" I hiss, even though Olivia couldn't possibly have seen what just happened over her shoulder.

"See what?" She frowns at me.

"Over there." I point to where the two are talking again, the pretty blonde with a smile on her face.

"I don't know what you're talking about."

The blonde reaches for her drink, and I know I can't sit here and do nothing.

"I'll be back." I jump to my feet and stride across the room, heading directly for the woman who has captured my attention from the minute she set foot in the room.

"Brody!" Olivia calls after me, but I ignore her.

I reach the woman as her wine glass touches her mouth, and I shove past the guy she's talking to, to reach her.

"Don't drink that," I blurt out, my heart thumping.

Her eyes narrow in confusion at me, but the glass lowers slightly from her plump lips.

"And why not?" she asks, her voice just as sexy as I expected it to be.

"I think he just spiked your drink."

I turn my attention to the douche she's with, but his face gives nothing away.

"Me?" he questions, his tone full of cocky outrage. "Don't be stupid."

He's good, I'll give him that, but I know what I saw.

"When she turned away, you put something in her glass."

He stands up from his stool, his posture staunch.

He's a tall guy, but I'm taller. I'm broader too, and he knows it as I watch him size me up.

"That's a big accusation."

It certainly is, and I could be wrong, but I really, really don't think I am.

I can't let her drink that.

"Please don't drink it, I'll buy you another one, just... don't, *please*?"

She eyes me curiously before shifting her gaze to the man she's been talking with for the past hour.

"Did you put something in my drink?" she questions him, holding the glass up in his direction.

"Don't be ridiculous, Mandy."

"It's *Morgan*," she bites back swiftly.

"Morgan, *sorry*." He grimaces and, if I'm not mistaken, he's starting to look a little hot under the collar. There's a fine layer of sweat over his forehead. "You don't believe this clown, do you?" He glares at me.

She looks between the guy who has been working hard to literally charm the pants off her, and me, a complete and total stranger.

I might not know her, but at least I'd never forget her name. What a fucking idiot.

"I saw him put something in there, I swear," I tell her softly. "I've got no reason to lie."

She watches me carefully for a few beats, before her gaze settles on her suitor. "You promise you didn't?"

He nods furiously.

She raises the glass to her lips, and I'm contemplating knocking it from her hand when she shoves it abruptly in his direction. "You drink it then."

"Wha... what?" he stutters.

She shrugs, her eyes gleaming. "If you didn't try to drug me, then *you* drink it."

"I ah... I don't like wine."

He tugs on his tie, his expression starting to look panicked.

"Pretend you do," she insists.

We've drawn the attention of half the bar now. Even the bartenders have stopped what they're doing to take notice.

He glances around nervously, all too aware that he's being watched.

She raises a brow at him as she waits for him to take the glass from her.

He reaches his hand out, and I don't miss the slight tremor in his fingers.

He's panicking.

He *definitely* tried to drug her. He looks guilty as hell now that he's being faced with putting that shit in his own body.

"Bottoms up," I prompt, crossing my arms firmly across my chest.

He tips the glass to his mouth and takes a small sip before setting it down on the bar.

"All of it," Morgan says without flinching.

He winces and lifts the glass again, this time downing its entire contents.

I don't know what he put in that glass, but I sure hope it was fast acting; I'm going to look like a fool if he walks away from here unscathed.

For a few beats nothing happens, and I start to wonder if my eyes were playing tricks on me, but then he speaks.

"See? I'm *fine*." He blinks slowly a few times, and it's obvious he's feeling hazy already.

I meet Morgan's eyes, and she sucks in a breath, her eyes wide. She can see it too.

The asshole tries to take a step towards her, reaching for her arm and stumbles a fraction.

"Fuckwit." I sneer as I shove him backwards. "Don't you fucking touch her."

I don't want him anywhere near her. Every part of me is screaming to keep her safe.

The crowd of people behind him move, and he falls to the floor, groaning.

It's not even half of what I want to do to him, but it's clear he's in no state. He can't even get up off the ground.

"Oh my god." I hear Morgan gasp from next to me. "He really tried to roofie me."

"Are you okay?" I pull my attention from the prick on the floor and rest my hand on her arm.

She nods, her green eyes wide.

I lean across the bar and catch the attention of the bartender. "Call the police, would ya?"

He nods quickly, his expression shocked. "Good catch, man, thank you."

I nod at him once before turning my attention back to the woman next to me.

"Morgan?" I question.

"Yeah."

"I'm Brody."

"Thanks, Brody," she whispers, her eyes fixed on the man that is now being dragged to his feet and out of the bar by two of the security staff.

"Anytime." I smile.

Olivia shoves through the crowd and tugs on the sleeve of my shirt. "Holy shit, that was insane. Are you okay?" she asks Morgan.

"I'm fine," Morgan replies, her voice returning.

"I'll be over in a minute, Liv," I tell Olivia. She nods, and heads back towards our table.

"Are you really okay?" I ask, my eyes travelling over her face and down to her sexy red dress. It's probably not the most appropriate time to be checking her out, but I can't help it. Her curves are smokin' hot.

"Thanks to you, I'm fine." She reaches out and lays her hand on top of mine. "Seriously, thank you."

I have to restrain myself to stop from flipping my palm so I can intertwine our fingers.

I don't know what to do now. I don't want her to think I'm hitting on her, but I also don't want to leave her here alone.

"Are you here with anyone?" I ask.

She shakes her head. "Just me."

"Do you have a car?"

She shakes again. "I took a cab."

"Come on." I tip my head in the direction of the table I've been sitting at, watching her all evening.

"Come where?" she questions, her expression curious.

"You're coming to sit with me, I'll get you a new drink – sans drugs."

She giggles softly. "That's very sweet of you, but I don't think your girlfriend would appreciate me crashing your date." She tips her head in the direction of Olivia who is still watching us with interest.

"Liv?" I question with a chuckle.

She nods.

"Well then, I guess it's lucky she's my sister."

CHAPTER TWO

Morgan

Oh *wow*. Can anyone say tall, dark and handsome?

Seriously, I don't know where this guy has been hiding, but I'm glad he's here now.

He's utterly gorgeous.

Deep, brown eyes, and thick dark hair, hell, even his beard is sexy.

I can feel the warmth of his big, warm hand on the small of my back, just above my ass, even through the fabric of my dress as he guides me through the crowded bar, over to the table where his *sister* – *not* girlfriend, is waiting for him.

I glance up at him, way up, because god he's tall, and he smiles down at me.

I should feel *something* about what just happened to me – I almost got drugged by some creep who would have taken me home and done things to me that I don't even want to think about – but all I can think about is the knight in grey jeans who swooped in and came to my rescue. Maybe I'm in shock.

I don't know how I'll ever be able to repay him for that, but I can think of a few ways I'd be willing to try, if I'm being honest with myself.

We reach the table, and he pulls out a chair for me to sit down in.

"So..." He leans down, his hands resting on the table next to me, and his muscular forearms flexing. He's got his shirt sleeves rolled up in that way that makes guys look one hundred times hotter instantly. "What do you want to drink?" he asks me softly, his voice husky.

"I'll have whatever you're having." I reach for my bag and pull out some cash, but his hand lands on mine, stopping me.

"I don't want your money."

"But I want to buy you a drink, you just saved me from that creep doing who knows what to me."

He flinches, but his hand doesn't move. It's so big it swallows mine completely.

"I don't care. I'm not taking your money." His dark eyes burn into mine, and I honestly can't even recall what point I was trying to make.

"Do I know you?" I ask suddenly, a feeling of familiarity washing over me that I can't quite put my finger on.

He shakes his head, a sly grin crossing his lips. "I think I'd remember meeting a woman like you."

His words make my heart beat faster and my palms sweat.

"Is a beer okay?" he questions.

I nod, still trying to settle my racing heart.

"Beer for you too, Liv?" He shifts his gaze to his sister who, honestly, I'd forgotten all about.

"Sounds good." She nods.

His hand lingers on mine for a moment longer and then he's striding over to the bar, his long, lean legs carrying him quickly.

I blow out a deep breath. I don't think I've taken a proper breath since I first laid eyes on him.

I smile at his sister. "I'm Morgan. I'm really sorry I crashed your evening."

She waves away my apology. "Don't be silly, and besides, he hasn't listened to a word I've said all night, he's been... *preoccupied*." She rolls her eyes.

I don't know what she means by that.

"Alright... well thanks anyway." I shrug.

"I'm Olivia," she tells me, and I really should have seen that they were related; she's tall too – not as tall as him, but I'm not sure *anyone* is as tall as him, and she's got the same dark hair and eyes.

"Did you know that creep?"

I shake my head. I'm actually kind of embarrassed about it. I don't get out much, certainly not dressed like this, and for good reason apparently. Look where it got me – being hit on by a guy that should be behind bars.

"Just met him. He was pretty full of himself, but I just thought he was cocky, you know? I never thought something like that would happen."

Brody arrives back at the table then, three beers in his hands.

It's kind of ironic really, after what just happened, that I'm so willing to take an open drink from a stranger, but when Brody smiles and hands it to me, I don't feel concerned in the slightest.

He didn't have to do anything about what he saw, but he did. He came to my rescue, and that makes me trust him, stupid as that might be.

He slides into the chair next to me, his knee bumping the table as he tries to fit his legs under, making the whole thing shake. "Sorry," he mutters, and I grin.

He's just so tall.

I've always had a thing for tall guys, and Brody is proving to be no exception.

"Thank you." I smile before taking a sip of the cool liquid.

I think I need this drink after what almost just happened.

"I talked to the bartender, gave them my details to pass onto the police. They're barring the dude for life, and I think the cops want to talk to you tomorrow, if you want to give them a call?"

I nod. "Did they arrest him?"

"Sure did. They might have to swing by the hospital before the cells though, not that the bastard deserves it."

He went down like a sack of potatoes. I shudder thinking about it. God knows what that drug was, or how much he used, but it was fast and obviously strong to take a guy his size down that way. I never would have had a chance.

I would have been out that door and then god knows where, doing whatever he deemed a good time.

I could have wound up dead in a shallow grave.

I set my bottle down and fiddle with the sicker on the side. "Seriously," I glance up to meet his eyes, which are already on me, "thank you for saving me. I don't know what I would have done if you hadn't seen."

"There was no chance of that happening," Olivia mutters, and Brody shoots her a glare.

I still don't know what she's talking about, but she seems amused at Brody's reaction.

"It was nothing," he says before he brings his bottle up to his lips and takes a long pull.

It *wasn't* nothing, not at all, but I don't know how to make him see that.

"I'm just glad I got there before you drank it."

I'm glad too, so unbelievably glad.

"What a psycho," Olivia grumbles. "Whatever happened to a guy actually being a gentleman?"

"We're not all bad." Brody smirks, and *damn*, I have to agree. He's not bad at all.

I didn't think the creep at the bar was too bad either though, a bit of a douche, but not the worst guy.

How wrong I was about that.

It just goes to show that I shouldn't be out here. I should be home, in bed or watching a movie. Something tame like that. Places like this bar chew up and spit out naive women like me.

"I think I should head off..." I tell Brody.

I'm suddenly feeling out of place and a little vulnerable.

"You okay?" he questions, his voice tender and his dark eyes gently probing mine.

It's sweet. *He's* sweet.

"I'm alright, I think it's just time I called it a night."

He nods in understanding.

"I'm going to call a cab." I reach for my bag.

"No." he replies quickly. "I've got my car; I can drive you home."

I shake my head, even though I so badly want to say yes. "I can't ask you to do that."

"You didn't. I offered. If you're comfortable with it, I'd rather take you myself than have you get in a cab with some stranger."

"You realise you're a stranger too, right?" I grin at him.

He chuckles and runs a hand through his thick hair. "I guess that's true, but still... I want to make sure you get home safe."

I chew on my lip nervously. I don't want him to go out of his way, but at the same time, I really *do* want him to.

"I live over on the east side," I warn him.

"I'm going that way to get home anyway." He shrugs easily.

"If you're sure?"

"Never been surer," he replies with a wink.

CHAPTER THREE

Brody

"It's just up here on the left." Her hand comes through the middle from the back and points up the street.

I indicate and pull my four-wheel drive BMW off to the side of the street just down from where she's pointed to.

It's a quiet area, and the house she's pointing out is a cute little bungalow.

There's a light on in the front window, so at least I know she's not going into a dark house.

"Thank you, again, for the ride," She says softly.

"It's no problem, I'll walk you up," I say.

I hear her protest, and Olivia's snigger, but I ignore them both and climb out of the car.

I open her door for her and hold my hand out to help her climb down – this might be a perfect size vehicle for me, but it's a bit of a nightmare for people that are normal height.

She gives me a heart-stopping smile as she places her hand in mine.

Her feet are firmly on the ground, and I still haven't let go.

She doesn't seem to mind as we stroll hand in hand towards her door.

"This is me." She shrugs her shoulder.

"Nice place."

"It does the job."

We're standing face to face, our joined hands between us, just staring at one another.

"You're okay to go in on your own?"

"I think I'll manage."

I chuckle. "Alright then, well I'll leave you to it."

"Okay... thanks again, for tonight. For the ride... and *everything*."

"Anytime. You sure you're okay?"

She giggles. "Stop asking me if I'm okay."

I grin and nod. "Sorry, I'm just worried about you."

She seems reluctant to walk away, and I want to kiss her, cup her jaw, pull her flush against me, but I won't. I'm just some guy she met in a bar, and she's been through enough for one night.

Our hands drop apart and I turn away reluctantly, heading back to my car.

I get about a metre away when she calls after me.

"That's it? No kiss? You've been giving me that *look*, and you're not even going to ask for my number?"

I chuckle and turn back to face her, walking slowly backwards. "I was trying to be a gentleman."

"What if I don't want you to be?" She pouts, her expression amused.

"Sorry, Morgs, my mumma raised me right." I chuckle.

She pouts. "So that's it then?"

I shake my head at her. "I'll call you."

"You don't have my number."

"I'll find you."

"It's a big city."

"I've got a head start."

"And what might that be?" she asks, her tone sassy, and her hands finding her hips.

I gesture up at the building behind her. "I know where you live."

She shakes her head in amusement. "Touché."

I watch her climb the few steps to her front door.

I jump into my car and start the engine, easing forward up the street slowly until I'm right outside her place.

"Can't you just go kiss her already, you've been drooling all night," Olivia grumbles.

I ignore her. I'm still too busy drooling.

Morgan has unlocked the door and is just turning the handle.

I lower my window and call out to her, "Hey, Morgs?"

She spins around, a smile on her face.

I hold out my cell and snap a picture of the large sign out the front of her house, the one offering her services as a real-estate agent. "Now I've got your number too."

"That's cheating," she calls back to me.

I smirk. "*Maybe*. But it works just as well."

She narrows her eyes in disapproval, but honestly, I think she looks pretty pleased with herself.

"You can go, you know," she says as she watches me idling in the middle of the street.

"I'll go when you're inside."

She rolls her eyes. "I'm right here, seriously, it's fine."

"Go inside, Morgan."

She looks like she wants to argue, and part of me almost wishes she would. I'll get out of this car and put her inside that house if I have to, but instead she smirks, shakes her head at me again and disappears inside the house with a wave.

I chuckle softly and head off down the street.

"Well... that was different," Olivia comments.

"Shut up."

"No can do, I'm afraid." She sniggers. "I've never seen you get all knight in shining armour like that before, what the hell was that about?"

I speed off across town, back in the direction of my place. Olivia lives on my way home – in the complete opposite direction to where we just dropped Morgan.

I raise a brow at her. "What? You think I should have let that prick spike her drink and say nothing?"

"Of course not." Her fist connects with my shoulder. "Don't be stupid. But the whole walk her to her door and wait while she goes inside is very nineteen fifties of you. Don't even get me started on the hand-holding and coy flirting."

"You're telling me that asshole you've been dating doesn't walk you to your door?" I attempt to change the subject.

"I'm not dating him anymore," she grumbles.

"And why not?" I grin.

She huffs out a breath. "Because he *was* an asshole."

I chuckle. "*Exactly*. And I bet he never made sure you got home safely."

She mutters something to herself, before switching the focus back to me. "So, are you going to ask her out or what?"

I shrug. "Maybe."

She groans. "Don't be *that* guy, you should text her. Tonight. No one wants to wait three days to hear if someone wants to see them again."

I'll definitely be texting Morgan. There's no doubt about that. I just like to wind my sister up – she makes it too easy.

I don't know if I'm grateful that I had Olivia with me tonight or not; on the one hand, it stopped me from taking things too far with Morgan, but on the other hand, it stopped me from taking things too far with Morgan.

Being a gentleman has never felt like so much of an effort as it did when I walked away from her.

"Don't worry, sis, you saw her right? There's no way I'm ghosting."

"You're such a guy." She rolls her eyes.

"What?" I chuckle. "Are you trying to tell me you didn't notice how pretty she was? Or that you didn't think she seemed nice?"

"Don't put words in my mouth, she was super-hot, and she seems cool, I like her. Even if she has dodgy taste in men."

I pull up at the curb outside Liv's place. "Are you talking about the dude from the bar, or me?"

She smirks as she swings the door open. "Who's to say I wasn't referring to both?"

"You're such a bitch," I retort.

"You know it. Thanks for the ride." She blows me a kiss, slams my door shut and strolls up the path towards her door.

She might give me shit for it, but she knows damn well I always wait for her to get inside. It's not just something I do for pretty girls I meet in bars.

I wait until her front door closes and a light comes on inside before driving away.

***

I tug my covers higher up my chest and stare at the glow coming from my phone.

I saved Morgan's number to my phone about a half hour ago and I've been staring at it like a chicken shit ever since.

It's been a while since I've wanted to ask a woman out on a second date – not that tonight in any way constitutes a first date, but still, it's almost the same concept.

I've been too busy the past three years with basketball to do any real dating beyond the scope of meaningless one-night stands.

I'm out of practice.

I could text Adam and ask him for advice – he's a serial dater – but it's likely to be 'treat 'em mean, keep 'em keen', or something equally as unhelpful and stupid.

I should listen to my sister. She's a female after all, and right now she's probably my best bet.

To: Morgan

From: Brody

Hey Morgan, it's Brody... from tonight... I just wanted to make sure you were alright?

It's so lame, but I can't think of anything better that isn't going to make me sound like a desperate loser, so I hit send, despite my better judgement.

I toss my phone on top of my covers and run my hands over my face.

I hope she replies; I really do want to see her again.

Maybe I should have asked for her number like a normal person instead of hijacking it from her sign.

I groan. I'm so shit at this.

My phone dings and I scramble to pick it up and unlock the screen.

It's from her.

The corners of my mouth lift into a grin.

To: Brody

From: Morgan

Hey Brody from tonight, long time no chat. I managed to get up to my bedroom and into my pyjamas with no further incident as luck would have it, thanks for asking. Did you manage to get in your pjs okay? x

I grin at her smartass response. I know I'm being oddly overprotective, given that she's a woman I know nothing about, but I can't stop thinking about her and what would have happened if I wasn't there tonight.

To: Morgan

From: Brody

No need. I sleep nude.

Her reply is almost instant.

To: Brody
From: Morgan
What I wouldn't give to be a fly on that wall...

I chuckle. I like this woman. She seems fun, light, free.

To: Morgan
From: Brody
You know, if you let me take you out on a date, you might get to see for yourself one day...

I fidget with the edge of my sheet as I wait for her response.
My screen illuminates, and I swipe it open as fast as I can.

To: Brody
From: Morgan
Are you asking me out on a date, Brody from tonight?

I grin as I tap out my reply.

To: Morgan

From: Brody
What if I am?

To: Brody
From: Morgan
Then I'd suggest you do it properly.

I chuckle.

To: Morgan
From Brody
Touché. You want to go out with me some time, Morgs?

Fuck, I don't know what's wrong with me, my heart is racing as I wait for her response.

She takes *forever* to reply, but when she finally does, the three words make me grin.

To: Brody
From: Morgan
I'd love to.

CHAPTER FOUR

Morgan

"For the love of god," I mutter under my breath.

I don't know what the hell takes a teenage boy so long to get ready, but I woke him over an hour ago and he's still not here.

"*C'mon*, Ethan, you put on shorts, a singlet and shoes, it's not rocket science. Do you really want to be late to your first training?" I yell.

"Coming, Mum!" he calls back down the hall.

I roll my eyes. Sometimes I still can't believe someone let me have the sole responsibility of looking after a human being.

I guess I've done alright, he's survived this long, and with little to no help from his father.

He bounds out of the room, the spitting image of the man who wants nothing to do with him most of the time, his height towering over me at only sixteen years old.

"Had to do my hair." He grins, his smile cocky and flicks his head, the hair he's spent the past god knows how long styling, sliding further back off his face.

"Oh, I bet your coach and the rest of your team won't care that you're late as long as your hair looks good."

He grins. "Thanks, Mum."

"For what?"

"You said my hair looks good."

I roll my eyes. "You're *unbelievable*, now get in the car before we're late.

"Another compliment," he croons as I push him in the direction of the front door.

He snags the water bottle I've filled for him from the bench as we pass and then jogs towards the door.

"You need to chill, we've got heaps of time."

I hate being late, I always do everything I can to be on time, a trait my relaxed-as-shit son didn't inherit apparently.

We finally get into the car and we're driving to the sports centre, Ethan rambling on and on about some new play he learnt at the training camp he went to last weekend, and how he can't wait to see Hunter again – a kid he met at the camp that has been selected for the Tigers youth team with him.

It's not that I'm not proud as hell of him for making this team, because I am, there's just only so much basketball chat one woman can handle, and I reached my limit about three years ago.

Ethan has always been obsessed with the game.

I think he's moved onto talking about the training schedule for the season, but I can't focus, I'm too busy thinking about the dark-haired man who swept me off my feet last night.

I've learnt the hard way not to expect anything from men, they only screw you over in the end, but it's hard not to see Brody as the perfect gentleman.

He was sweet, considerate and protective.

Not to mention the fact that he was completely gorgeous.

He's way out of my league, but he seems interested, so I'm not about to let him in on that little secret.

"Just pull up out front, Mum and I'll meet you back here after," Ethan instructs as he points out the door to the building.

"Nice try, kiddo, but I'm coming in to sign the permission forms, then I'll be out of your hair, I promise."

He groans as I pull into a park – he's a typical teenage boy – doesn't want his mummy going anywhere with him, but that's just bad luck for him. He's only got one present parent, so I'm the only option he's got.

He's been even less impressed with me showing up at school and sports events lately since I overheard some of his mates calling me a 'MILF' – that was both flattering and *incredibly* inappropriate.

"Hey, there's Hunter," he says as he glances around.

He swings his door open and jogs off, bouncing a ball in front of him as he calls out to his friend.

"I'll just see you in there then," I mutter.

I grab my bag and lock the car before heading into the busy gym.

This is the Tiger's gym – the main team trains and plays here along with the youth teams, so Ethan has been buzzing about the possibility of getting up close and personal with some of his idols. The Tigers are his favourite team, and they've managed to get an ex player to coach the boys this year, much to the excitement of my son and his friends.

Coach Owens is all I've heard about for the past three weeks.

I find the desk set up with the administration and fill in all the necessary forms for Ethan to play the season.

I glance into the gym; the large group of boys are all running drills, orange basketballs flying around in some type of organised chaos that extends beyond my hand-eye capabilities.

I notice a group of women – the mums if I had to guess – standing off to the side, watching something that *isn't* their children, with interest.

I know I should leave and let Ethan do his thing, but they're all here, so I figure staying for a few minutes can't hurt.

I approach the women nervously. I've never had much luck making friends with many of the mothers from Ethan's schools over the years – most of them look at me with their noses turned up – because of my age, or something else, I'm still not sure, but I've only managed to have a conversation with a handful of them. It's been better since we moved out here, but I still wouldn't say I had many real friends.

I had Ethan young – really, *really* young – and while I'm not ashamed of it anymore, it wasn't the easiest time of my life, and I still get judged on it often.

"Hey," I say as I reach them, waving awkwardly, and surprisingly, I'm met with smiles and a chorus of hellos.

We exchange pleasantries and inform one another of whose son is who. One or two of them only look a few years older than me.

Hunter's mum, Isabella, recognises Ethan's name as I say it, and she smiles wider at me.

"What are we all looking at here?" I ask her.

"Oh, sweetie, have you not seen the new coach?" she fans her face dramatically.

I laugh. "No, is he hot or something?"

She grins knowingly and points in his direction. "He's so handsome it's making me blush from all the way over here."

I giggle as I follow her finger with my eyes.

There's a group of men, most of whom look middle-aged and slightly overweight, there's one younger-looking guy but the back of his jacket says medic, so that's not him... I'm about to ask who she's talking about when I see him.

Clipboard in hand, whistle around his neck, a head of thick, dark hair, the most handsome face I've ever seen.

I swallow deeply.

Brody.

Coach Owens.

Brody Owens.

I *knew* I knew him from somewhere.

I watch him blow the whistle and point to one of the boys, instructing him to try something differently.

"Oh *wow*," I breathe.

"*Oh wow* is right," Isabella agrees.

I can't believe this. The only man to ever treat me like I'm something valuable, the only man to ask me out on a real date in years, and he's my son's new coach.

Brody blows his whistle and yells at the boys to do a lap of the building.

They toss the balls and run for the door, racing one another.

One of the balls rolls in our direction, and I break away from the group to retrieve it.

I bend down to stop it rolling at the same moment that a large basketball shoe lands on the top.

"Thanks, I got it," the voice tells me as he snags it from the floor.

I glance up at him, slowly straightening to look at the man who I know that foot belongs to.

"Morgs?" he asks in confusion as he recognises me.

I can't help but love the way he says that. My dad called me Morgs when I was a little girl, but that doesn't make this situation any less weird.

He's probably wondering if I'm some crazy stalker who has followed him here.

"Hey," I squeak. "So, I guess *you're* Coach Owens?"

He nods slowly, his expression still confused. "Sorry, are you here to see me or...?"

"It looks like my son is on your team," I squeak.

His eyebrows shoot up. "*You* have a son?"

I bite on my bottom lip and nod.

"You didn't tell me that."

"You didn't tell me you were a basketball coach."

"Valid point." He nods slowly, clearly still thinking this whole thing through.

"I didn't tell you a lot of things... we don't exactly know one another, remember?" I remind him.

His brow is furrowed as he tries to make sense of this new information.

"Sorry, you're going to have to talk me through this... your son is how old?"

I bury a giggle. His confused face is cute.

"Sixteen."

I know what he's thinking... if my son is sixteen, then how old am I?

"Are you sure he's your son, because no way in hell do you look old enough to have a kid that age."

I shrug, a smile playing on my lips. "Pretty sure he's mine. I gave birth to him if I remember rightly."

He chuckles, the frown fading and morphing into a smile. "How old are you, Morgs?"

I could tell him that asking a lady's age is rude, but he'll find out eventually – if he still wants to date me after this revelation, that is.

"Thirty-two…" I shrug a shoulder. "I had him young."

A devilish smirk graces his gorgeous face. "Damn, Morgs… you are one hot fucking m—"

"Shhhh," I hiss, a giggle bubbling from my lips. "You can't say that here."

"It's my team." He grins wider. "I can say what I want, whenever I want to say it."

"The other mums are watching," I say, my eyes darting out to check and, sure enough, all eyes are on us.

"Let them watch." He chuckles, his gaze never leaving mine.

We stand there almost awkwardly, sexual tension radiating, not saying a word.

I hear the sound of pounding feet – the boys are back in the gym.

"Another lap," Brody yells loudly without even looking up.

I hear a chorus of groans, but they do as they're told and leave the gym again.

"So… I'm a single mum… is that a problem for you?"

His lips turn up into a sexy smirk, his head slowly shaking. "No. It's not a problem for me."

I like that. I like it a lot.

"Okay... well... *good*," I reply lamely.

"I better get back to it," he says as he bounces the ball in his hand, causing me to jump.

He chuckles as he turns, going back to his practice.

"Bro— Coach Owens," I say before he gets too far away.

He glances back at me over his shoulder, and god he's so sexy I can't deal with it.

"How old are you?"

"Same age as you," he answers before dribbling the ball, his long legs carrying him back to the side of the court.

I watch as he does some tricky-looking move with the ball before shooting at the hoop from well outside of the three-point line. The ball swishes through the basket.

"Pretty smooth, slick," I mutter under my breath.

He turns back, and the look he gives me takes my breath away.

"Wow," I breathe, my pulse thrumming as I walk back on shaky legs towards the group of women who are all gawking at me like I've grown an extra head.

I can't believe *he's* here.

I suddenly wish I'd worn something nicer than ripped jeans and a white t-shirt. I haven't done my makeup and my hair is piled on my head in a loose knot, tendrils floating messily around my face.

He probably can't believe I'm the same woman from the bar.

"Well that looked awfully cosy," Isabella teases as I re-join the group.

"I ah... actually sorta know him a little bit," I admit. "I didn't know he was their coach though."

I figure there's no point in bullshitting. A group of women like this could sniff out gossip a mile away.

"Pllleeeease tell us you went out with him so we can all live vicariously through you," one woman says at the same time another asks if I've seen him naked.

I giggle nervously. "No and no... not yet anyway."

That sets off a chorus of ooooohs and giggles so loud that Brody turns around from the group of boys who have finished their run and gathered around him.

He pulls a baseball cap onto his head backwards and smirks at us, that sexy god damn twist of his lips that makes my belly flip.

Christ.

I need to get out of here before I do something that will give my son *real* reason to be embarrassed.

CHAPTER FIVE

Brody

I shoot the ball at the hoop and it hits the back board before dropping through the net.

I roll my shoulder out, trying to ease the discomfort. I've only been messing around with Adam for about twenty minutes and it's already playing up.

He retrieves the ball and lazily dribbles it to the free throw line.

"How were the cubs today?"

He's dubbed my team the cubs. Technically they're the Tiger youth team, but I guess cubs works just as well.

"Strong. Solid." I nod. "We made some good selections this season."

He nods and tosses the ball towards the hoop. It sails through effortlessly.

He's not the top point scorer in the country for no reason.

"I saw a few leaving; I would have killed to be that height at sixteen."

I huff out a laugh. Adam towers over most normal people, and I doubt he was any different in his teenage years.

I bounce the ball I collected from the court after his basket and toss it back to him for another shot.

"It's a good team, should be a successful season if they keep focused."

If I *can keep focused* I should be adding to that sentence, because, *damn*. I've never felt more distracted than I did this morning when I knew Morgan was watching me.

"You'll keep them in line."

"I'm taking one of the mums on a date," I blurt out.

The ball sails through the air as he makes another three-point shot.

"Fuck, bro, you don't muck around."

I chuckle. "I actually met her last night – *before* I knew she was one of the boy's mums."

He throws his head back and laughs. "That kid is going to get it big time from his teammates if you shack up with his mother."

He's probably not wrong, but that won't stop me.

Her kid – *Ethan*, he's a good player. Hopefully he's got thick skin.

Adam grabs another ball off the rack and bounces it in front of him. "Since when are you into cougars anyway?"

"Dude. She's not a cougar. She was a young mum."

"Step-daddy Brody. I could get used to calling you that."

"Blow me," I retort.

"Only if you ask nicely." He chuckles, a shit-eating grin on his face.

I shake my head in amusement and hold my hands up for him to pass me the ball.

My phone sounds loudly from the benches as I make the shot – it hits the rim and misses.

I jog over and grab my cell, grinning when I see the text is from Morgan.

"I see you and that smile; you've caught the bug." Adam howls with laughter as he jogs for the discarded ball.

I flip him off before unlocking my screen.

To: Brody
From: Morgan
You're a liar, Brody from last night.

I don't know why, but her message makes me grin wider.

To: Morgan
From: Brody
I resent that, Morgs. What have I lied about?

To: Brody
From: Morgan
I googled you, you're only 29.

I chuckle. So maybe I am a liar, just a little bit. I'm also ecstatic to hear that she cared enough to look me up online; it gives my ego a boost.

To: Morgan

From: Brody

So? What about it?

To: Brody
From: Morgan
I'm 32, I'm way too old for you.

To: Morgan
From: Brody
Bullshit you are.

To: Brody
From: Morgan
You're only 13 years older than my son!

I smirk as I type out my response.

To: Morgan
From: Brody
You're only 16 years older than your son.

I wait and wait, but unlike her previous messages, a reply doesn't come instantly. I'm just about to toss the phone back into my bag when it alerts me she's finally replied.

To: Brody
	From: Morgan
	Touché.

I chuckle loudly.

"So, you're pretty sweet on this chick?" Adam says from behind me, and I jump.

"Fuck's sake, quit lurking around."

He chuckles, his grin wide and easy. "No can do. So, who is she? Is she hot? Where'd you meet her?"

He fires off the questions in rapid succession, leaving me no opportunity to actually give him an answer.

I cross my arms across my chest, my shoulder protesting slightly.

"That all you want to know?" I question.

"For now."

"Her name is Morgan, she's a solid ten out of ten, and I met her when I went for a drink with Liv last night, some douche was about to spike her drink."

"For real?" His brows shoot up, his grin fading.

I nod tightly. "Prick would have taken advantage of her too. I don't even want to think about it," I mutter.

"Was she okay?"

I hide my smile. Adam is a big teddy bear – he's all tough on the exterior, talks a lot of shit, but I'd trust him with my life – and more importantly, I'd trust him with people I care the most about.

"She was fine. I got to her before she drank any of it."

"Did you kick his ass?" he growls.

"No need actually... she made him drink it." I smirk. I'm fucking proud of the way she handled the situation.

"She *what*?" He howls with laughter.

I nod. "I know, it was epic. He faded like the sack of shit he is and then we had him arrested."

That reminds me, I need to follow up with that, see if the police need anything more from me.

"She sounds badass. You sure she wants to hang around with a washed-up schmuck like you?"

I shake my head in amusement, pick up my gear bag and tug my cap onto my head. "You're a shitty friend," I call over my shoulder as I stroll out of the gym.

"You know you love me!" he yells after me.

***

To: Morgan

From: Brody

I just got off the phone with the cops, they said they've got everything they need to charge the guy. I wasn't sure if you knew.

As much as it made my stomach turn having to think about what his intentions might have been, I went over it all with the detective leading the investigation. They're taking it seriously at least. Apparently, the bar had footage of him spiking her drink – so there's no way he'll be getting out of it without conviction. Morgan shouldn't even have to testify or anything.

My eyes are fluttering closed with sleep when I'm startled awake by the phone still clutched tightly in my hand.

To: Brody
    From: Morgan
    Thank you for following up. I went in this afternoon and spoke to them about it. They really couldn't believe how lucky I got... if you weren't there, it would have been a different story.

My throat feels thick reading her words.

To: Morgan
    From: Brody
    Well I was there. Let's not talk about what could have happened, it makes me want to break into that scumbag's house and beat the shit out of him.

To: Brody
From: Morgan
Are you always this protective?

I'm not. I know that. I don't know what it is about this woman, but she makes me want to beat my chest and throw her over my shoulder.

To: Morgan
From: Brody
You bring it out in me, Morgs.
So, about that date, can I take you out for dinner tomorrow night?

To: Brody
From: Morgan
I thought you'd never ask.

CHAPTER SIX

Morgan

"I can't believe this is happening, this is worse than the MILF comments." He fake gags. "You know this is scarring me for life, right?"

He's such a drama queen sometimes.

"Trust me, this is *not* worse than your underage mates perving on your mum."

He mutters something incomprehensible under his breath.

"Look, just don't make it awkward and I'm sure Brody won't either – the guys on the team never even have to know."

"They all saw him talking to you yesterday. One of them said he was looking at you like he wanted to—"

"I do *not* want you to finish that sentence," I interrupt him. "*Ever*," I clarify. "Do you understand? *Jesus*, why are kids so inappropriate these days?"

The little shit has the nerve to laugh. "*Whatever*, but just remember, you're the one dating my coach. You're the picture of inappropriate right now."

"Can't you go play your PlayStation or whatever it is? Since when do you lurk around in the living room on a Saturday night? Call one of your mates to come over or something."

"You know what? I think it's just since you started dating my coach."

I groan. The kid is impossible. I love him to death, but most of the time I just seriously want to see if the hospital he was born in offers some type of refund policy.

"Go away."

He laughs. "Nah, I think I might just hang around a while... say hi to Coach Owens."

He strolls away, and I hear him rummaging around in the fridge. That's the other thing with teenage boys, they're always eating something, anything... *everything*.

"If you embarrass me, I'm grounding you for a week!" I yell after him as I peek out the front curtain again, checking to see if Brody has arrived yet or not.

"Now you know how I feel," I hear Ethan mutter from the kitchen.

God, give me strength, I'm nervous enough about this without having to deal with my child's sass.

He leans against the door frame, half a sandwich in his hand.

He frowns at me. "Where's your jacket?"

"Shit. I forgot."

I glance at my watch. Brody should be here any minute.

I rush off down the hallway to my room and rummage around in the mountain of clothes that didn't make the cut for tonight until I find my jacket near the bottom.

I'm just shrugging it on when I hear the doorbell and Ethan call out, "I'll get it."

Fuck my life.

I take one last glance in the mirror and rush back down the hall, pausing to catch my breath before stepping into the living room.

I can hear the two of them talking and I hope like hell that Ethan isn't saying anything stupid.

"We'll work on it at Tuesday's practice, but I think you'll get it, your skill base is solid," I hear Brody saying.

"Yeah?" Ethan asks, and I can hear the excitement in his voice. He likes this praise from Brody. I see the pleased look on his face and can't help but think that he likes Brody in general, no matter how much he's been pretending to hate the idea of me dating him.

"Hey," I say, and Brody's eyes snap from my son to me.

"Wow," he breathes, "you look incredible." His eyes sweep over me from head to toe.

"Um thanks," I reply, my nerves getting the better of me.

It's a much tamer compliment than the one he gave me at the gym yesterday, but with my son right here listening to every word and watching every move, it all seems like too much.

"You ready?" he asks as he hitches his thumb over his shoulder, his bicep flexing in the fitted black t-shirt he's wearing.

I nod eagerly.

He turns to Ethan. "Good to see you, bud, I'll have her home by midnight."

Ethan would roll his eyes if I said something like that, but he laughs at Brody. "Keep her all night if you want."

I blush and shoot him a 'what the fuck' look.

"Sorry, that came out wrong." He flicks his hair back from his face again.

I hate the way he does that; he's going to give himself whiplash one of these freaking days. Not to mention it looks ridiculous. I don't think he got the memo about the old-school Justin Bieber haircut being out of style.

"Just bring her home when you're finished with her," he amends.

"Ethan!" I hiss as Brody chuckles.

"Fuck," Ethan cusses. "I mean, shit, I mean... that's not what I—"

"Just go inside, stop speaking and stay out of trouble," I instruct, my cheeks flaming red.

"I'll see you at training, Coach Owens," he says quickly before shoving me out the door and shutting it behind me.

"Well... that was awkward."

"Was it?" Brody teases. "I didn't notice."

He holds his arm out for me to take and I do.

He leads me down to his huge SUV and opens the door for me. "You really have this gentleman thing down pat," I compliment him.

"I thought you didn't want me to be a gentleman?"

His grin is cheeky and wide. I can see more of his face today; he's trimmed the beard that was rough and unruly just yesterday.

I like it like this. He looks so sexy.

"Maybe I lied. There's always a time to be a gentleman," I say as I climb into his car, using his hand for assistance.

"A gentleman in the streets and a freak in the sheets?" he questions with a chuckle.

"Absolutely." I sigh, my teeth sinking into my lower lip.

His laughter dies off as his eyes trail over my lips, a hungry look in his eyes.

"You alright there, slick?" I whisper.

He blinks, breaking the trance and chuckles easily again, his hand running through his thick, dark hair. "I'm good."

He shuts my door, and I watch as he jogs around the front of the hood. I've never seen a guy make running look sexy before, but low and behold – Brody has managed it.

"Where are you taking me?" I ask as he fastens his belt and pulls out onto the street.

"My place, if that's okay with you?" He glances at me before looking back at the road.

I like the sound of that far too much.

I should be being cautious. I shouldn't be in the car alone with a stranger, going to his house where we'll be all alone, but Brody doesn't feel like a stranger. He feels like someone I already trust.

"Sounds perfect, are you cooking for me, Coach Owens?"

He chuckles. "Not if you want to get through the evening without getting food poisoning. I'm not much of a cook."

I giggle. "At least you're honest."

"I've ordered Italian. I hope that's okay with you?"

"You're doing it again." I smirk.

He meets my eyes for a fraction of a second. "Doing what?" he questions.

"You've gone from asking if I'm okay, to asking if what you've planned is okay."

He chuckles. "Maybe I'm nervous."

I like that he's nervous.

"I'm nervous too," I admit. "But I love Italian food."

He reaches over with his hand and lays his huge palm over mine.

I like the feel of it far too much. It might be a simple gesture, but it feels comforting, safe.

Everything about Brody makes me feel safe, and that's a scary concept, given how little I know about him.

I glance at the window and see where we are. I frown as we drive through town and back out the other side.

"You're such a liar!" I cry when I figure out what's happened.

"What?" he asks, his tone surprised.

"You don't live anywhere near the east side, do you?" I demand.

He chuckles as he realises what I'm referring to.

"You came completely out of your way to drive me home the other night."

He shrugs. "A little white lie never hurt anyone."

I can't believe he did that for me.

I tug on the zip of my jacket. "Why are you being so good to me?"

He stops at an intersection and turns to face me, his brows raised. "I haven't done anything any decent guy wouldn't have done, Morgs."

"Maybe I don't really know any decent guys then," I whisper, shrugging my shoulders.

His eyes narrow and he swallows deeply, a displeased expression on his face. "Well you do now." He grounds out the words and they send a tingle running down my back.

His hand tightens around mine, squeezing gently. "You're safe when you're with me. I won't let anyone do anything to hurt you. Alright?"

I meet his dark eyes, and I can see that he means it. He's thinking about that creep in the bar again, and it's obvious he's barely holding it together.

"Thank you, slick."

His posture relaxes and he eases forward from the intersection. "Are you going to tell me what I did to earn the nickname 'slick' or do I have to guess?"

I giggle. "You went a little heavy on the hair gel."

He chuckles. "Liar. I don't even own hair gel."

He's right, I'm a terrible liar, his hair is perfection. It's just begging to have my fingers run through it.

"It was those slick moves on the court yesterday, Coach, I know you knew I was watching."

"Hell yeah I did." He chuckles. "I might not be able to cook, but I sure as hell can play ball, well... I could before anyway."

He pulls into the driveway of a huge, flash house and hits a button to open the garage door.

He parks inside and climbs out with a grin.

I unclick my belt and wait for him to come to my door; he does, swinging it open and holding his hand out to help me down.

I'm average height, but I feel tiny around his huge frame.

I reach for his hand, but at the last second, he changes his mind, instead leaning further forward and gripping my waist and lifting me clear off the seat, then setting my feet on the ground.

I gasp as he stares down at me, his hands still resting on my waist.

"Um, thanks," I breathe.

"You're welcome," he replies, his voice gravelly as his eyes roam over my face.

He's so handsome I can barely remember how to breathe. His intense stare is causing my belly to summersault like crazy.

He blinks, his eyes soften, and his hands drop almost as though he didn't even realise he was still touching me.

He chuckles and shakes his head like I'm a puzzle he can't figure out. "Let's go inside."

CHAPTER SEVEN

Brody

She takes a sip of her red wine, and I watch the action like a wild dog would watch a piece of meat being waved under his nose.

Jesus. I can't say I've ever referred to a woman as a piece of meat before, and I don't want to start now, but *shit* she's so tempting.

She's a beautiful woman, but more than that, she's funny, smart and interesting to talk to.

She's flirty and fun, and I feel like I could spend all my time with her and it still wouldn't be enough.

"Tell me about your injury," she prompts. "Are you planning to go back next season?"

I shake my head and sit my beer down on the coffee table next to the open containers of Italian food.

I had intentions of setting the table nicely, with candles and that kind of shit, but apparently, take-out is meant to be eaten from the containers, on the couch – according to Morgan anyway.

"It was career ending," I explain. "I tore all the ligaments and tendons, ripped some of them clear off the bone... My shoulder is never going to be back to how it was before, despite some of the finest sports doctors and surgeons in the country giving it their best shot."

She looks at me sadly. "I'm sorry."

I shrug. "It happens, it's not like an injury is uncommon in basketball. Goes with the territory."

"I know, but you were at the peak of your career, that has to suck."

I smirk at her. "What do you know about my career?"

She nibbles on her bottom lip and tucks her legs up further under her ass. "Not a lot to be honest. Not enough to be able to know where I recognised you from." She narrows her eyes at me and grins. "But Ethan has talked about you nonstop since he got named in the team. It's been 'Coach Owens this' and 'Coach Owens that' twenty-four seven. He's probably watched every game you've ever played, and I've heard all the commentary while I sit there reading a book."

I throw my head back and laugh. "Sorry that we bored you that much."

She blushes slightly. "I'm not much of a sports girl, but my son didn't seem to get the memo."

"He seems like a really good kid," I say, nudging her knee with mine.

She smiles softly. "He is, for the most part. No one ever tells you how much work teenage boys are."

I chuckle. I certainly was no walk in the park for my parents at that age, so I feel for her, I really do. There are a lot of conflicting hormones at sixteen.

"I think this team will be good not only for his basketball skills, but for him as a person too – he can use all the positive male influence he can get."

"His dad isn't around?" I question, asking the question that's been niggling at me since I found out someone had put a baby in her belly.

She sighs heavily. "*Nope*. I mean he's drifted in and out over the years, whenever he has time or inclination. He always pays his child support these days – so I guess that's more than some fathers."

That angers me. I can't think who in their right mind would walk away from a woman like Morgan, I sure as hell wouldn't, especially not if she was holding my child.

"Was he young too?"

I probably should mind my own business, but I'm curious.

"He was seventeen when Ethan was born. He wasn't around for much of the pregnancy or the birth. In fact, I don't think he met Ethan until he was nearly one."

"He sounds like an asshole."

She giggles. "He was. He *is*. I cut him a lot of slack back then because neither of us planned to have a baby at that age, and I didn't want to ruin his life, you know?"

I know what she means, but her logic is all messed up – that baby was as much his responsibility as he was hers, and she shouldn't have been left to do all the work.

"My tolerance kinda ran out when he started cheating on me while I was heavily pregnant though..." she carries on, shrugging as she speaks. "We broke up, his parents shipped him off to some fancy school far away, and eventually he just stopped calling regularly. Barely came over when he was in town, and that was it really. He pays money into my account every month and he drops in about once every year or so... sends Ethan a card on his birthday with a hundred bucks in it if he remembers... He rings Ethan's cell sometimes I think, but Ethan doesn't usually say much about it."

The guy sounds like a total wanker.

"Does he have any other kids? A wife?"

She looks at me curiously. "You know, that's a really good question, and one I haven't thought to ask."

She sighs again and I feel bad for bringing this all up.

"I'm sorry, it's not my business."

She smiles. "It's fine, honestly, it's no secret and I'm well and truly past being disappointed for myself – I only hurt for Ethan now. Chad is a lot of things, but father of the year isn't one of them."

"His loss," I say as I reach for her hand and take it in mine.

She turns her palm face up so our fingers can intertwine.

I huff out a laugh of disbelief as she shuffles a little closer to me.

"What's so funny?" she asks curiously.

I bring her hand up to my lips and kiss it softly. "I just can't believe that some idiot had *you* and his son, and he let you go."

She tugs that sexy bottom lip into her mouth and nibbles on it, a light pink blush staining her cheeks. I know my praise is making her nervous, but I don't care.

She might not be used to hearing compliments from her asshole ex, but she better get used to hearing them from me, because I'm planning on giving them out often.

"Enough about him, let's talk about us."

"About us?" she questions.

"Yeah... how would you say this date is going on a scale of one to ten?" I ask as I twist our joined hands in front of us.

"Well the food was delicious, but not home-cooked, so that's a deduction. A nine for food."

I chuckle. "I should get a bonus point for *not* cooking for you, trust me."

She giggles. "Fair point, bonus point taken into consideration."

I slide closer to her.

"The conversation has been great, but you did make me talk about my ex, so..."

"Hey! You said it was okay."

She laughs, her whole face alight with amusement. She looks so happy, sitting in my living room, flirting with me.

"Fine." She rolls her eyes. "You can have an eight-point-five for conversation."

"Eight and a half?" I reply, outraged. "My chat is at least a low nine."

I tug on her arm, pulling her closer; we're almost flush against one another now.

"Nine, absolute max." She grins wickedly.

That's it, I'm going to have to fight dirty.

I turn so I'm facing her and almost press our bodies together, the hand that isn't holding hers cups her face, and I hear her gasp at our close proximity. A slight tilt of my head and I'll bring our lips together.

"What about chemistry, where do I rate on that scale, Morgs?" I whisper hoarsely, my breath fanning her face.

I tip my chin slightly, pulling back only just before our lips meet.

Her eyes flutter closed, and she sighs breathily. "Eleven," she whispers.

A deep chuckle falls from my lips before colliding with hers in a passionate kiss, the way I've wanted to do ever since the moment she walked into that bar looking so fucking sexy.

She drops my hand and threads her fingers into my hair, tugging roughly on the strands.

Her plump lips move with mine, opening slightly to allow my tongue to run over them.

A rumble comes up my throat, and I have to physically stop myself from lifting her the way I did earlier and depositing her into my lap.

I don't want to be the guy that takes it too far too soon.

She makes a soft moaning noise and my resolve slips further. My hands find her hips.

"*Brody*," she whispers longingly, and I pull away, just enough that I can think straight again, gasping for air.

"Jesus, Morgs, you know how to make a guy lose his mind."

She giggles softly, her hands dropping from my hair to my shoulders.

"I think you have the same effect on women."

Her hands lightly trail down my chest before falling onto her lap as she leans back.

"I was beginning to think you were never going to kiss me," she teases as she gets to her feet, grabbing her empty wine glass as she heads for the kitchen.

"That was one time." I chuckle. "I was being a gentleman."

"It didn't feel like you were being a gentleman just now," she calls from the kitchen.

I chuckle and run my hand through my now-messy hair.

"I'll tell you what though, slick, I give you an eight for kissing."

"Eight?" I call back, jumping to my feet and stalking after her.

I find her in the kitchen, a devious smile on her face as she sets down the wine bottle.

"What?" she asks innocently, batting her long lashes at me.

I take a step towards her and she takes one backwards.

"You'd give me an eight for that spine-tingling kiss in there?" I growl, taking another step, she backs up again until she's flush against the wall.

"I think you can do better." She tugs her lower lip into her mouth again.

"I'll show you better."

I step into her body, grab her legs and hoist her up into my arms before she can even say another word.

She gasps and I swallow it, dipping my head and kissing her without restraint until I have to come up for air. I suck in a breath and move on to her neck, kissing every patch of skin available to me.

She moans, louder this time, and I press her harder into the wall.

"Ten." She pants. "I give you a ten."

"Only a ten?" I grunt, bringing our faces level.

"Fifteen, twenty... one hundred..." she stutters. "I'll give you any number you want if you kiss me like that again."

I chuckle. I'm only too happy to oblige.

CHAPTER EIGHT

Morgan

It's been days since I've seen him, but I swear I can still feel where his lips touched mine.

Where his hands gripped my thighs...

If he can kiss like that, I can only imagine what a man like Brody Owens can do in the bedroom.

Of course, he was too much of a gentleman to let me find out.

He left me wanting, but also in awe of his considerate nature and respectful attitude. If my son grows up to be anywhere near as respectful towards women as Brody is, I'd be a happy mother.

He drove me home and walked me to the door with a PG version of a goodnight kiss, in case prying eyes were on us, which I'm confident they were.

The minute I stepped in the door, I was greeted by my teenage son, an amused expression on his face and a comment about Brody being an ass-kisser for having me home on time.

There is seriously no pleasing that boy, but I know one thing, the minute he starts dating, I am going to embarrass him big time – he owes me.

I take another sip of my coffee and try to wake myself up.

Brody and I spent half the night talking on the phone. He told me about how he's settled into his role as coach, and I told him about the real-estate business. He told me about his sister and all the things he used to do to her when he was younger, and I told him about what it was like having a toddler on my eighteenth birthday while all my school friends were out partying. He told me about his pre-game superstitions, and I told him how I still sleep with the hallway light on.

We talked about everything from total nonsense, to the more important things in our lives until I must have fallen asleep.

I woke up with the phone on the pillow next to me and a goodnight text from Brody waiting for me.

I've got to show three couples through a house this morning and meet with two new clients this afternoon about getting their properties on the market.

I'm exhausted from the lack of sleep, but oddly, I've never felt so alive.

Ethan bounds into the kitchen, his hair perfectly styled in that look he's going for, and his signature basketball singlet in place. He's got a Tigers hoodie draped over his arm. I swear the kid just has ten of the same items of clothing that he wears on repeat.

"Did I wake up in the twilight zone or are you ready on time for once?" I make a show of glancing at my watch.

He grins as he swings open the fridge and starts loading food into his backpack. "Lachie's mum is giving me a lift to school this morning," he explains.

I resist the urge to celebrate. Not having to drive him to school means I get a few extra minutes to sit in my kitchen and enjoy my coffee.

"I've got basketball practice after school today, don't forget," he reminds me as he fights with the zip on his overstuffed bag.

There's no way I'd forget, not when his coach looks like that.

"So, you're getting a ride there, and I just have to pick you up at six, right?"

"Preferably from in the carpark." He grins, before turning his back on me.

I flip him off when he's not looking. Little shit.

"Say hi to Brody for me," I say as he strolls out of the room, in an attempt to rile him up.

"Not a chance in hell, Mum," he calls back.

I laugh as I hear the door open and he calls out goodbye.

"Teenagers," I mutter as I put the milk back in my now-half-empty fridge.

I swear that kid is going to send me broke one of these days.

I glance at my watch again, slug back the rest of my coffee and think energetic thoughts as I walk out the door to my car.

***

By the time I pull into the carpark of the gym just before six, I'm grateful to be there; I've felt oddly on edge all day, like someone was watching me. At one point, as I drove between clients, I could have sworn a flashy white sports car was following me, but by the time I decided to get its number plate, it was gone.

I've always had an overly active imagination; it would seem I let it get the better of me today – must be the lack of sleep.

I glance around the carpark. There are some players, maybe nineteen years old or so, milling around the entrance, and that makes me feel better about getting out of my car and crossing the darkened carpark on my own.

The weather is packing in; I can feel the drops of rain hitting the top of my head as I rush across.

I wrap my jacket tighter around myself as I step into the gym. The group of swooning mothers is nowhere to be seen today, so I don't go right in, instead choosing to watch from the viewing window in the foyer instead.

I spot Ethan in a line of boys, running drills. I watch as he catches the ball, dribbles it before making a long-range shot, which he nails. He flicks his hair back off his face and jogs to the back of the line.

I scowl at the back of his head. That god damn hair, I might have to cut it off while he sleeps.

My eyes wander until they land on Brody. He's working one-on-one with a tall – even by basketball player standards – teenager. He's explaining something to the boy, and when he complies and completes the move as explained, I see Brody's mouth turn up into a satisfied smile. He claps the boy on the back – praising him.

He's wearing a singlet and a baggy pair of basketball shorts. His arms and shoulders are toned and defined.

Even marred by his surgery scars, he doesn't look like an ex-athlete; he looks like one in his prime.

He blows the whistle loudly and points across the gym and the team takes off running.

His eyes follow them, but as they pass the window I'm watching from, his gaze catches on mine and he smiles, wide and easy.

I raise my hand and wave, my teeth sinking into my bottom lip as I stare at him in all his glorious perfection.

He waves back, his grin somehow widening further.

He holds up one finger to me, asking me to wait, and I nod eagerly.

I busy myself looking at the team photos that adorn the walls on the foyer. I stroll past year after year until I find one from three years ago, and I scan it, looking for Brody. I find him in the second row, his arms crossed tightly over his chest.

I trail my finger over the shape of him. Basketball has never seemed so interesting.

I hear the gym doors open and then a flood of chatter and bouncing balls as the team make their way out of the gym.

Teenager after teenager file out, some of them taking a seat, others heading straight out into the carpark.

Their mothers must be able to follow instructions.

Poor Ethan.

I spot my son sauntering out of the gym; he scans the foyer, finds me and gives me one of those chin lifts, before turning back to his conversation with the boy I now know is Hunter.

Too cool for his mum, yet again.

I roll my eyes and go back to looking at the team photos, wandering further behind the huge wall of them. I find Brody in three more; he's got the same staunch pose and defined muscles in all of them.

"Something catch your eye?" a deep voice near my ear startles me.

I spin around and scowl at Brody, who is chuckling to himself.

"You scared me." I shove his chest.

He catches my hand and tugs me towards him, surprising me by placing a kiss to my forehead.

We're out of view of the kids around here, but still, I'm surprised he's being so publicly affectionate.

"Sorry, Morgs, you were kind of in the zone."

I smirk at him. "I was just checking out a pic of some hot ball player."

"Oh yeah?" He chuckles, his arms weaving around my waist and pulling me flush against him.

"Yeah." I nod. "His name is Adam, he's the lead point scorer," I tell him innocently, relaying the information he told me last night about his friend and former team-mate.

"That wounds me." He groans, a cheeky smile on his lips. "Makes sense though... you're too pretty to be dating me without an ulterior motive."

I shake my head in amusement. "I know, right?" I tease.

He chuckles again and I feel the deep rumble through our joined chests.

He lowers his head to my level and brushes his lips softly against mine.

I feel eyes on me again, and when I peer around Brody's side, I see they belong to my son.

"Gross," he deadpans. "You two should get a room."

Brody turns at the sound of his voice. "Really, dude?" he asks, his brow raised. "You *want* me to get a room with your mum?"

I smother a laugh. Brody is being an awfully good sport when it comes to dealing with my son – I guess he's used to dealing with a whole bunch of teenage boys; one is probably a walk in the park.

"Wha— no, I... that's not what I meant," Ethan stutters, his cheeks reddening. "You guys need to stop twisting my words."

"Are you ready to go?" I ask him as I try to tug away from Brody, who doesn't let me move an inch.

"I'm ready." He hitches his bag higher on his shoulder, his eyes narrowing on us. "Do you have to do that here?"

I open my mouth to say something, but Brody gets in first.

"Sure do, bud, I'm planning on making it a regular thing. Is that going to be a problem?"

Ethan crosses his arms across his chest, and I can physically see him thinking it over. "Might be."

"Anything I can do to sweeten you up?" Brody offers, the corners of his mouth twitching as I glance up at him.

"Are you bribing him?" I ask at the same time that Ethan replies, "Bribery, I like it."

"You bet I am," Brody says, to me this time. "I want to kiss you whenever I want, I don't care what it costs me."

I huff out a laugh.

"Within reason," Brody amends, releasing my waist with one of his hands and pointing a warning finger at Ethan. "Just because you're my strongest point scorer, doesn't mean I'm going to let you off easy."

I see Ethan's chest puff up ever so slightly with Brody's praise.

Apparently, I'm not required for this conversation. It seems Brody and Ethan are going to work this one out on their own.

My son likes this man, I can tell – he looks up to him, and the thought warms my heart.

"I want you to take me to a Tigers game. Courtside tickets," Ethan replies, his tone smug, like he thinks Brody won't be able to deliver.

I feel a little guilty at his request. I've been promising him tickets for years, but it's never happened. They're not exactly cheap.

"Done," Brody replies simply.

Ethan's eyes bulge. "Seriously? You get to kiss my mum and shit and I get to go to a game?"

"*Ethan*!" I hiss. "You're making it sound like you're my pimp."

He swipes his hand in my direction, effectively brushing me off. "Shhh, Mum, I'm negotiating."

Brody chuckles, and I feel his lips brush against the top of my head.

"Name your terms," Brody offers easily.

"I want to bring a friend."

"Done."

"And I want snacks."

I roll my eyes, but Brody just laughs and nods. "Of course. Goes with the package," he reassures him.

Ethan nods thoughtfully and I resist the urge to stomp my foot.

"Are we done here?" I demand.

Ethan nods. "Deal."

Brody slips his other hand from my middle and closes the gap between him and my son.

"Deal." He offers his hand and Ethan shakes it firmly.

"Thank god," I mutter under my breath.

"I'll pick you up tomorrow at seven," Brody announces, glancing back over his shoulder at me."

I frown in confusion. "For what?"

"The basketball game." He shrugs. "The Tigers play tomorrow night and it sounds like we're all going to the game."

Ethan whoops loudly and throws his arms in the air. "Seriously, Mum, your new boyfriend is the man," he yells out before rushing off, I assume to celebrate with whoever is left here from the team.

I gape at Brody as he strolls back over to me. "You realise you just made his year, right?"

He shrugs. "It was no big deal."

I step towards him and throw my arms around his neck. "It was a very big deal, slick." I press a kiss to his jaw. "Thank you."

"What kind of boyfriend would I be if I didn't deliver the goods?" he asks with a smirk.

I feel myself blush. "Sorry about that, I don't think he realised he was jumping the gun."

He silences me with a kiss. "Don't apologise, I like the way it sounds," he whispers against my lips.

My head feels foggy and my heart beats fast as he claims my lips with his again.

CHAPTER NINE

Brody

"You know what, Coach Owens? I think it's cool that you're dating Ethan's mum, maybe then he'll actually get some game time."

I glance in the rear-view mirror in time to see Ethan punch Hunter in the arm and reply, "Better get your mum to date the assistant coach or something or you'll be keeping the bench warm all season."

Hunter is a centre – probably the best the team has got.

I shouldn't laugh at the two of them giving each other shit, I really shouldn't, but I can't help it.

They remind me of myself and my teammates when I was their age.

"Give it a rest you two," Morgan tells them, but I don't miss the hint of amusement in her tone.

They laugh, shove each other some more and then I see them take an earbud each and start bopping their heads to some song they've deemed worthy of listening to.

I chuckle and look back at the road.

"Oh to be sixteen again."

"I can't say I'd be in a rush to go back to my sixteenth year," Morgan replies with a sigh, "I had swollen ankles and a baby on the way."

"Sorry, Morgs, I didn't mean—"

She giggles. "I know, slick, you're fine."

I swear sometimes that my injury was to my brain and not my shoulder, because I can't believe I just said that.

"Thank you so much for this, Ethan hasn't been able to sit still since you told him we were going tonight."

I grin, grateful for the subject change. "Honestly, it's not a big deal, I feel like you're giving me too much credit. I get free tickets from the team."

"It doesn't matter. You're going to be his favourite person for the next year."

I glance in the rear-view mirror again, but the boys are paying us no attention.

I like the sound of being Ethan's favourite person. Probably too much given the early stage of mine and Morgan's relationship – if this can even be classed as a relationship yet. I want Ethan to like me, because I really like Morgan and I have a feeling that if her son hated me, I wouldn't have a shot in hell.

It's a weird situation when I think about it. If I weren't Ethan's coach, I doubt I would have even met him yet; Morgan doesn't strike me as the kind of woman who rushes into things, certainly not regarding her child.

"I hope this is okay," I blurt out suddenly, "you know... we've only been on a couple of dates and I'm already spending time with your son... I don't want you to feel like it's too much too soon."

"You're his coach." She laughs lightly. "And I'm hardly going to pull him from the team – he'd kill me."

"You know what I mean, we can keep the two separate... I don't have to be involved with him outside of the team if you don't want me to."

She reaches over and takes my hand in hers, gently stroking the side of my palm with her fingertips. "I'm comfortable with whatever Ethan is comfortable with, slick, and I think you're forgetting that he was the one who negotiated these terms, he didn't just ask for tickets... he asked to go to a game *with you*."

Huh. I suppose he did.

"He likes you, Brody, I can tell. So, if it's not too much for you, then I'm more than okay with it."

I squeeze her hand. I like hanging out with Ethan, he's a good kid. Morgan has done an amazing job with him.

"It's cool, Coach, stop making a big deal about nothing," Ethan says from the back, and my eyes widen when I realise he's been eavesdropping. "You're the first boyfriend Mum's had that I actually like."

The little shit was listening to every word.

I clear my throat. "Alright, well... ah... *cool*."

I glance at Morgan out of the corner of my eye and she's biting down on her lip to stop herself from laughing.

I point a warning finger at her. "So, you've had other boyfriends then?" I ask, my brows raised.

"Uh-uh, slick, we're *not* talking about that." She giggles with a shake of her head.

"There was Nick," Ethan answers for her, "the guy was a total douche."

I chuckle as he carries on speaking, naming the few men who have dated his mum, Morgan getting redder and redder by the second.

***

"I can't believe you got *Adam Burton* to come to our next training," Ethan crows. "Lucas and Jeremy are going to bust a nut."

"Can you *not* say that?" Morgan grimaces as I pull up outside her place. "I don't need a visual of anyone's nuts."

We dropped Hunter off on the way, but Ethan has not stopped talking the entire trip back; he's humming with excitement at just the idea of Adam being at practice.

Morgan wasn't kidding – I think this might be the best night of the kid's life.

Not only did we see the game courtside, but I took them into the changing room after to meet some of the guys.

I've never seen two teenage boys so excited about something that didn't involve half-naked women.

It was tough, being back in that changing room with my old team, and not getting to be a part of the action, but it was worth it to see the look on Ethan's face.

"But they will," he exclaims, leaning through the centre of the seats to grin at her, his hands making an exploding motion.

"Just say thank you and go inside." She groans.

"Thanks, Coach, that was the coolest, seriously." He holds his fist out to bump against mine.

I comply. "You're welcome, and can you call me Brody when we're not at practice or games? Coach makes me feel like I have to be on my best behaviour or something."

He's half out the car, and I'm not even sure he's listening. "Sure, sure," he says, before he slams the door and takes off up the path.

"I could have sworn I shut that gate when I left." Morgan frowns as she watches Ethan jog through the already-open gate.

I frown at it. "Maybe someone came to visit while we were out... left it open?"

"Maybe." She shrugs and a smile returns to her face. "No one ever comes to visit me though."

"I do."

"Is that a hint that you want to come in?" She glances back at her house and watches Ethan unlock the door.

"It sure is." I smirk. "So, are you going to invite me in, or not?"

Her gaze lingers until Ethan turns on the light, I don't know why, but she seems a little bit on edge.

"Are you okay, Morgs?"

She grins, wide and easy. "I'm good... overactive imagination..."

I'm about to ask her what she means by that when she says the magic words I've been dying to hear.

"Wanna come in for a drink?"

CHAPTER TEN

Morgan

"Remind me again why this is a good idea?" he asks, the shot glass of tequila pausing at his lips.

"Live a little, slick." I grin, the warmth of the alcohol has settled into my limbs, making me feel relaxed and confident. "Or I can go get you a beer if you're not up for a little fun?"

The way he keeps looking at me is taking effect too; I feel heated from head to toe when his dark eyes appraise me like that.

"On three," he growls, and I grin victoriously. "One, two..."

"Three," I finish before I lick the salt on my hand and toss the shot back.

I squeeze the juice from a lemon slice into my mouth as the liquid burns its way down my throat.

Brody chuckles as he squints from the sour taste. "I'm not doing another one of those fucking things." He shakes his head as he springs from the couch. "I don't care if it makes me a pussy. I'm getting myself a beer."

He strolls into my kitchen, looking completely at home. I like that. I want him to feel comfortable here.

"Get me one, would you?" I call after him.

"What's the matter, Morgs? Too much tequila?"

"Never," I retort, "but I'm worried I'll do something stupid if I have another one."

He appears in the doorway again, two beers held casually by the necks in one of his hands, a sexy-as-sin smirk on his face. "Can't say I'm not intrigued by that."

"You would be." I roll my eyes as I take the beer he's offering me.

He slides into place next to me, lightly cupping my jaw as he settles. "Do something stupid, Morgs... live a little," he teases me with my own words.

I want to do something stupid, *and* reckless, and I *really* want to do something that involves dragging him upstairs to my bed.

Those deep, dark eyes of his pierce into mine and hold me in place.

His face moves, and he brushes his lips over mine in the most featherlight of touches.

"Oh shit, sorry," Ethan says from behind me. "I just wanted to get a drink. Hey, are those shots? Are you doing *shots*?"

I groan at the unwanted interruption and feel Brody's mouth curve up into a grin against mine.

He places one more chaste kiss to my lips, and his hand falls from my face.

"Apparently your mum is pretty big on the shots." Brody chuckles as he slings his arm casually across the back of the couch."

Ethan snorts out a laugh of disbelief. "Can I have one?"

I scowl at him. "You're sixteen remember, buddy, drinking age is eighteen."

He rolls his eyes and picks up the tequila bottle to inspect it. "All my mates are allowed to have a drink at home," he grumbles.

I mull it over for a minute, a lesson my mum taught me once flitting through my mind. She caught me and my friend trying to buy a pack of smokes when we were underage. Much to my surprise, she bought them for us – and then proceeded to make us smoke the entire pack. I've never touched a cigarette since, my mouth tasted like an ash tray for about a week afterwards.

"Alright." I shrug. "*One* shot."

"Yeah?" Ethan asks, brows raised.

I nod and hold out a shot glass to him. "Fill it up."

Brody chuckles and buries his face in my neck as Ethan fills up the small glass right to the top.

Ethan looks at me expectantly.

"Well, down it goes," I prompt him. I don't tell him about the salt or lemon – this one is going down straight.

He brings it to his mouth and tips it down his throat in one go, swallowing it.

I almost wonder if I've got this particular lesson wrong, but then he gags, as the alcohol tries to make its way back up his throat.

"Why the hell do you drink that?" he moans, before gagging again. "That's so gross. I feel like I'm gonna puke!"

Brody laughs deeper against my skin.

"Welcome to the world of drinking," I tell him smugly.

"No thank you," he grumbles as he stalks off to the kitchen, a disgusted expression on his face. "I'm not drinking that shit ever again."

Brody straightens up and holds out his palm for a high-five. "I'd call that a parenting win."

I giggle and press my hand against his. "He's a teenage boy, he'll be likely to forget he ever said that in about two weeks' time."

"Gross, it won't go away," he moans from the kitchen.

We both laugh.

The rummaging in the fridge stops and Ethan strolls back out of the kitchen, his hands loaded up with food.

I'm almost too scared to go into his room these days; it's probably filled with dishes and mouldy leftovers.

"Night, Mum... night, Coach. I mean Brody," he corrects himself quickly. "Thanks again for tonight, it was awesome."

His eyes light up at just the thought of it.

"You're welcome, man, I'm glad you had a good time," Brody replies.

"Night, Eth," I say.

Ethan nods once and then disappears from the room. I feel like the worst mother in the world for thinking it, but I hope like hell that he doesn't come back down here.

Brody's eyes lock on mine again the minute we're alone, and I feel that same familiar rush of heat, right down to my toes. "Where were we?" he almost growls.

He doesn't seem at all bothered by the interruption of my son, and that only makes me want him more.

I don't know if it's the alcohol making me brave, or the fact that we've spent the entire evening hand in hand as I've watched him dote on us, that makes me feel confident to climb into his lap and straddle him.

His hands find my sides, grazing over my hips as his eyes smoulder. "You're too sexy for your own good," he growls.

A giggle slips from my lips. I don't think of myself as sexy, but when he's looking at me like that, it's a hard notion to deny.

He thinks I'm sexy – and that makes me feel it too.

I run my hands through his hair and his eyes flutter closed.

Who would have thought after the incident in the bar, that I'd end up being saved by a handsome-as-hell knight, and then find myself in his lap, wanting to kiss him so badly it hurts?

My hands slide from his hair to his jaw and his eyes open again. I don't know what he sees when he looks at me, but I can't even think about it before his lips are on mine, his hands around my waist, tugging me even closer against his firm body.

He's all toned muscles and defined ridges. He might be a coach now, not a professional athlete, but his body definitely didn't get the memo.

My hands explore his arms as his tongue explores my mouth.

I pull away, breathing heavily. "Stay the night with me," I pant.

I want him close to me, and not just because I'm still feeling on edge, or because he's drunk too much to drive, but because I want him here – with me.

I can't imagine walking him to the door and saying good-bye to him right now.

He brushes a long strand of curly hair behind my shoulder. "You want me to stay the night?"

I nod, nibbling my lip as my nerves finally settle in – I guess a few shots only get you so far.

"I'll be the perfect gentleman," he promises.

"Don't be," I murmur before I claim his lips again.

***

I'm in the bathroom, drying my hair off when I hear my phone ringing from the bedroom. I'm totally naked from my shower and given that Brody is yet to see me without clothes, I'm not about to give him a show now.

"Brody? Can you answer my phone?" I call out to him.

"Got it," I hear him reply before he answers, "hello, this is Morgan's phone…"

I hunt out another towel and wrap it tightly around myself.

"Sure, I'll just get her for you," I hear Brody tell whoever is on the line.

I rush out of the bathroom and take the phone he's holding out for me. "Who is it?" I whisper.

He shrugs. "Some guy."

I roll my eyes. I don't know why work calls can't wait until after ten on a Saturday.

I bring the phone up to my ear and Brody grins wickedly as he pretends to tug on my towel.

I swat his hand away and he chuckles.

"Hello, this is Morgan," I speak into the phone, my eyes still fixed on the shirtless, sexy man who is now reclined on my bed.

No one answers.

"Hello?" I ask again.

No reply.

I pull the phone from my ear and see that the call is still connected.

"Hello? Is anyone there?" I ask again.

The line goes dead.

"They hung up," I tell Brody.

"Call them back," he replies lazily, his eyes on me.

I don't want to call them back, I'd much rather go and lie down with him, but given my barely covered state, that might not be the best idea.

I hit a few buttons on my phone, but the number is a private one, so I can't even return the call.

He sits up straight and holds his arms out, gesturing for me to come to him.

I toss my phone on the chair in the corner, the mystery caller already forgotten as I stroll towards him.

He tugs me into his lap, my ass perched on one of his thighs and my legs draped over the other.

My fingertips trail over his bicep to his shoulder and come to rest around his neck.

He really is the sweetest man. He handles me with such care and tenderness, yet there's an air about him that lets me know that he won't put up with any shit – that he could be rough and protective if he needed to be.

"Are you telling Ethan I stayed the night? Or do you want me to sneak out the window?"

He nestles his face into my neck, his rough facial hair scratching me in the most delicious way.

"I'm not going to hide you – he's sixteen, I don't think he's a child anymore."

"You wouldn't be saying that if you overheard some of the conversations those boys have in the changing rooms." His eyes sparkle with amusement.

"I'm not sure I could think of anything worse." I giggle.

"So, we don't hide?"

I shake my head. "We don't hide."

His grin is so blindingly gorgeous, I know I've made the right decision by welcoming him into our lives. Things are moving fast, but I don't care, and it doesn't seem that he does either.

"Can I grab a shower?" he questions. "I've got some clothes and stuff in my car, I might go get something clean."

"So, you're not rushing off then?" I ask hopefully.

"Wasn't planning on it."

"Good," I whisper as he kisses my forehead.

He lifts me with little to no effort and sets me down on the covers.

He grabs his keys off the table on the far wall and strolls out of my room, still wearing only a pair of jeans, and without a care in the world.

I fan my face. That ought to get the neighbours talking.

I dress quickly and rush to the living room so I can peek out the front curtains and watch the show for myself.

I muffle a giggle with my palm as Brody catches me looking and flexes his bicep.

I glance at a car parked across the street, it looks familiar, but I can't place where from. It also looks expensive, too expensive for this neighbourhood.

"You really like him, don't you?" a voice comes from behind me, and I jump.

I drop the curtain and step in front of it as though that's somehow going to stop my son from knowing what I was staring at.

"Huh?"

"*Brody*." He laughs. "You really like him."

"Maybe." I shrug. "Is that alright with you?"

I might like to pretend that my decisions aren't affected by Ethan, but honestly, if Ethan hated Brody, I know I wouldn't have the desire to continue a relationship with him.

I'm not looking for a new dad for my son or anything like that, but it would be nice for him to have a male around that wasn't a complete moron.

"Yeah, Mum." He rolls his eyes in the way I've been told makes him look like me and scuffs his toe against the corner of the rug. "I like him, he's nice to you, he likes basketball, and he got me tickets to a Tigers game." He grins. "*Of course* I like him."

"I like him too," I admit.

"Knew it."

"Well aren't you just so smart." I grin at him.

"As long as he doesn't end up treating you like Dad does, I'll be happy," he grumbles, his eyes narrow as he thinks about his father.

I nod. I'm not sure what I could possibly say to that.

He might be a smart little shit sometimes, but he'll be a good man. I know that much. He's not his father's son – he's mine.

"Speaking of Dad—" Ethan starts to say, but he's interrupted by Brody coming back through the front door, still shirtless.

"Friendly neighbours," he says with a smirk.

I give him a pointed look. "Oh, I bet, you probably gave Betty from two doors down a heart attack."

"New house rule," Ethan pipes up, pointing a finger at Brody. "You have to be wearing a shirt at all times."

"Oh, c'mon now," I tease, "let's not make any hasty decisions... seems like bad form to cover up a sight like that."

Brody chuckles. Ethan groans. I laugh.

"I'm going out," Ethan replies, already heading for the door, "I'll be at Lachie's."

"Eth," I stop him, "was there something you wanted to tell me?"

He started telling me something, but then it was all abs and toned biceps, and my mind got a little scattered.

"Nothing that can't wait," he replies easily, without looking back.

He grabs a basketball from the ground and disappears out the door without a proper goodbye, just a wave over his shoulder.

"I'm going to shower," Brody says.

My eyes graze hungrily over his exposed skin. "I think that's a good idea." If he stands there looking like that for too much longer, I won't be responsible for what happens.

"Will he be out all day?" Brody asks, tipping his head towards the door Ethan just walked out of.

I nod slowly, my attention still on his body.

"Good. Then you're coming to lunch with my sister."

I feel my lips turn up into a smile.

I like the sound of that.

CHAPTER ELEVEN

Brody

"Liv, you remember Morgan, right?"

I press my hand firmer against the small of Morgan's back, guiding her closer to the table that my sister and my best mate are sitting at, waiting for us.

If Morgan didn't look so good wearing that dress she's got on, I might not have had such a hard time keeping my hands off her, and we probably would have got here with time to spare.

But no. She had to walk out looking like that, the black dress hugging her in all the right places, and her wavy blonde hair falling down her back. She looks like an angel. A sexy fucking angel.

"*Of course,* I remember." Olivia gives a look that says, 'are you stupid or something?', before turning her attention to Morgan. "You look hot."

I breathe in deeply through my nose. I was expecting inappropriate comments from Adam, not my sister. "*Olivia.*"

Apparently, sisters never stop being a total pain in the ass.

Morgan giggles. "Um, thanks... so do you."

Olivia pops a brow and glares at me. "Are you suggesting she doesn't look hot?"

I shake my head at her, a smile doing its best to lift my lips. "She looks hot as fuck, now stop being so awkward."

I glance at Morgan, and she's chewing on her bottom lip again, her eyes meeting mine. It doesn't help the situation in the least.

I try not to groan.

"I'm Adam," Adam says as he gets to his feet. He holds his hand out and Morgan takes it, shaking it.

"Morgan," she replies.

I pull out a chair and gesture for Morgan to sit down.

Adam sits too, and I watch as his gaze darts from me to Morgan and then back again.

Morgan didn't come into the changing rooms with me and the boys last night, so this is the first time the two of them have met.

"I met your son last night, right?" Adam questions.

"Ethan, yeah." She nods. "Thanks for being so good to him and his friend. I don't think you know how pumped they are that you're coming to a practice."

"I am kind of a big deal." He smirks, his arrogance fake – this time at least.

"Yeah, yeah, you're a real superstar," Oliva says sarcastically as she lifts her coffee to her mouth. "We're all so fortunate to be in your presence."

Olivia and Adam have a love-hate relationship. They love nothing more than pissing the other off. It's almost the same as mine and Olivia's relationship... maybe my sister just likes to argue with people.

I leave them bantering back and forth as I slide my arm around Morgan's chair. "You want a coffee, Morgs?"

"I'd kill for one," she replies softly, glancing up at me.

"I'm not sure where you normally get your caffeine fix, but I think you can just exchange them for money here. No murder necessary."

"Oh ha, ha," she replies, rolling her eyes.

It's hard to think she's older than me when she does that – it makes her seem so young.

A waitress comes over and takes our order before disappearing out back.

"So... Morgan..." Adam starts.

I groan and grab Morgan's hand on top of the table. "Prepare yourself for an interrogation," I warn her.

Adam scowls at me. Morgan giggles.

"*Morgan*," he starts again, "what do you do for work?"

"I'm a real-estate agent."

"Cool." He nods. "You live around here?"

"The east side."

I see her scowl at me as she answers that one.

He nods thoughtfully. "You got a thing for guys who can't make a decent shot?"

I chuckle and flip him off.

He grins and leans back lazily in his seat.

"Oh, I don't know," Morgan replies, "he doesn't seem to have any problems *scoring* when I'm around."

Adam's eyes widen a fraction in surprise before he bursts out laughing. "Oh, I like you, Morgan. I'm going to have some fun with you."

I resist the urge to reach across the table and punch him. Morgan just grins, her eyes dancing with amusement.

"I might have some fun with you too, hot shot."

Adam goes from looking smug, to looking a little concerned. I chuckle.

If Morgan can make the ever-so-cocky Adam Burton look worried, then she's just gone up another rung in my book.

"Two points to the new girl," Liv drawls.

The girls exchange a grin, and it makes me smile too. I like the idea of them being friends – I've got the impression that Morgan hasn't got a lot in the way of friends.

"I'm just going to shoot to the bathroom," Morgan says, rising from her seat. I stand with her, I'm not even sure why.

"You know where it is?" I ask, stepping forward to show her.

She smirks at me and presses her palm flat against my chest, pushing me gently. "I think I'll manage to find it, slick."

"You sure you'll be okay?" I ask again, this time teasing her.

"I think I remember what to do." She teases as she strolls away, leaving me standing there like an idiot, staring after the sway in her hips.

I drop into my chair when she disappears from sight.

"Oh man, you are so screwed." Olivia laughs. "I knew it was bad the other night, but that look on your face assures me it's ten times worse than I originally anticipated. You've got it so bad for her. I think you just met your future wife."

I don't even get to answer her before Adam cuts in, putting his two cents' worth in.

"You know, I thought you were bullshitting me about her being a ten out of ten, but damn." He whistles low. "She's too pretty for a critter like you."

Oliva laughs as I throw a packet of sugar at my so-called best mate.

He laughs. "But seriously though, she need glasses or something?"

"Fuck off."

"Only if I get to take your girlfriend with me."

I flip him off. "I swear hanging out with you takes about five years off my maturity level."

"No argument on the 'girlfriend' label... *interesting*," Olivia cuts in.

I breathe in deeply. I'm getting it from all angles today.

"Nope. Her son bet you to that one," I reply.

"Step-daddy Brody got the son on board." Adam grins. "High-five."

"Blow me."

"I've told you, only if you ask nicely."

"I'm having a hard time remembering why we're friends," I drawl.

He shrugs. "Beats me."

"All jokes aside, you look really happy when she's around, I like seeing you happy," Olivia says.

I glance at her before staring at the table, maybe I *do* prefer the teasing after all.

"Thanks," I mumble.

"Me too." Adam raps his knuckles against the top of the table. "It's about time you found yourself a woman."

I smirk at him. "That's rich coming from you."

He takes a sip of his coffee and grins. "Don't sweat it, I'll just marry your sister one day when I'm done having my fun."

Olivia glares at him and I laugh loudly.

"What's so funny?" Morgan asks as she slides back into her chair.

I open my mouth to tell her, but a hand landing on her shoulder stops me in my tracks.

She twists around to see who's touching her and all the colour drains from her face.

"*Chad*?" she asks, shock colouring her tone, "what are you doing here?"

Chad... *Chad*... I can't think why I know that name, but it's in there somewhere.

He reaches for her and she stands in a rush. He kisses her cheek and I hate it. I really fucking hate it.

"I was in town. I just saw you walk across the room and I couldn't leave without saying hello."

He's tall, blonde and broad-shouldered. If I was into guys, I'd call him handsome. He looks just like... *Ethan. Shit.* This is Ethan's dad.

Morgan falls back into her chair, and I can see her leg bouncing nervously.

"Holy shit, you're Chad Jenson, aren't you?" Adam blurts out, getting to his feet with his hand already outstretched.

I swallow deeply. *Chad Jenson.* Football superstar.

This is Morgan's loser ex?

No wonder he doesn't have any problem paying child support. The guy was virtually plucked straight out of high school and put on the path to become a professional athlete.

Chad turns towards Adam and shakes his hand firmly. "You play for the Tigers, right? My son's a big fan."

His eyes dart to my face as he says the words 'my son'.

I don't like the possessive tone he uses. It sounds like a warning. I know in that moment that he knows who I am – suspects at least that I'm with Morgan – he must have been here watching us for longer than he's letting on.

"That's me," Adam replies.

I hear Olivia introduce herself, but I'm barely paying attention to them, I'm more concerned about Morgan.

"Oh my god," I hear her whisper and my hand finds hers instinctively.

Chad turns back towards Morgan and me, but unlike Adam, I don't stand to meet him.

He looks expectantly at Morgan. "Are you going to introduce me to your friend?"

"Ah... sure... um..." Morgan stutters. I don't know who the fuck this guy thinks he is, but I already hate him, not only for how he's abandoned Morgan and Ethan, but for the way he's stripped Morgan of her confidence instantly.

It doesn't sit well with me.

This man intimidates her; that much is obvious. It makes my throat feel thick and my fists twitch with the need to connect with something.

"I'm Brody Owens," I answer for her. "Morgan's boyfriend."

His brows rise, just ever so slightly as I speak.

"Ah, the famous Coach Owens," he replies, extending his hand to me, and it all makes sense to me then... why he's here – he's been talking to Ethan.

"The one and only," I drawl.

I'm being rude as fuck, staring at his hand but not taking it, but frankly, I want to make him sweat.

He glances at my hand and frowns.

"You must be Morgan's ex," I add on, finally reaching for his hand.

He chuckles arrogantly. "I'm not sure I'm reduced to being just her ex..."

I'm pretty sure he is, but I don't reply. I won't give him the satisfaction of seeing me get angry.

He drops my hand, and I drape my arm around Morgan's shoulders, tugging her closer to me for comfort.

"So, where is my boy?"

"*Ethan* is at his friend's place," Morgan replies, her voice taking on more confidence now.

Chad nods. "I guess I'll catch him later."

"You're not just passing through?" Morgan asks warily.

He shakes his head and grins. It looks creepy and sly to me, but I doubt I'm being a great judge of character right now – I hate the guy already and I don't even know him. "I'll be around a while. Thought I should spend some time with my son."

Morgan huffs out a breath and mutters, "No fucking shit," under her breath.

I smirk.

"Well you've got his cell number," she replies.

"I certainly do." His eyes wander from her to me again and then he glances across the room like he's looking for someone. "I should go, I'll call you later?"

"I think Ethan's old enough to make his own plans now, Chad."

He shrugs, and the look of arrogance on his face makes me want to leap to my feet and remove it for him. "Maybe I'll call you anyway." He winks and I see red.

Morgan squeezes my hand and I blink, relaxing a fraction.

He begins to stroll away, but stops, glancing at the woman pressed against my side once again. "You look good, princess.

I've missed you," he says before turning away and striding across the room.

I watch him until he leaves, anger radiating from me. Olivia has her mouth hanging open, and Adam is eating something I didn't even see get delivered to our table, totally oblivious to any tension.

"Are you okay?" I ask Morgan through clenched teeth.

She glances up at me, eyes wide. "I'm not sure."

"*Chad Jenson* is your ex-boyfriend?" Olivia demands.

Morgan groans. "Yeah, but when we were teenagers, he was just *Chad* – not some football legend."

"That is *so* cool." Olivia swoons.

"The guy is a total jerk, Liv, there's nothing cool about him," I growl. "I don't think it's particularly *cool* to never spend time with your son, *or* to turn up unannounced and intimidate his mother."

Olivia rolls her eyes. "He was just saying hello, you're such a jealous little brat. Why don't you just pee on her? That ought to mark your territory."

"Can you do it after I'm finished eating? I don't want to get kicked out mid-meal," Adam asks.

I chuckle. I can't help it. Some more of the tension leaves my body.

I kiss Morgan's forehead. "You want to talk about it later?"

She nods, her mouth smiling, but her eyes still swimming with confusion.

I don't like any of this – she looks torn, and I don't know what it is that's got her feeling so conflicted.

CHAPTER TWELVE

Morgan

I wait until Brody has gone to the bathroom to pull out my phone and text Ethan. I'm fairly confident he's been talking to his dad, but I need to know exactly what he's said.

This isn't the first time Chad has shown up and tried – and usually succeeded – to scare off a boyfriend of mine. There was even one time that I was grateful for the intrusion – it saved me the hassle of an awkward break up, but I don't think I want him anywhere near Brody, no matter how unbelievably good-looking he might be, because there's no point in denying it – Chad has grown into a gorgeous man.

It's just a shame that he hasn't got the heart to match.

I tap out a quick message.

To: Ethan

From: Mum

Did you know your dad was in town?

He must have his phone glued to his hand because he replies so fast I almost miss it.

To: Mum

From: Ethan

Yeah... sorry, Mum, I was going to tell you this morning, then Brody came in and I didn't know if you wanted to talk about Dad in front of him.

I glance in the direction of the bathroom, but there is still no sign of Brody.

To: Ethan
From: Mum
Did you tell him about Brody?

To: Mum
From: Ethan
I told him you had a new boyfriend.

To: Ethan
From: Mum
Ethan! Why on earth would you tell him I was seeing someone?

To: Mum
From: Ethan
I wanted him to get jealous and feel like crap.

To: Ethan
From: Mum
Your father isn't going to be jealous that I'm dating.

To: Mum
From: Ethan
Really? Because he sure sounded pissed.

I refrain from groaning.

To: Mum
From: Ethan
I'm sorry, Mum, I was just mad at him for never showing up... do you think he's going to mess everything up?

That question saddens me so much – I wish my son didn't have to think of his father that way, I wish he could rely on him... that he could feel secure in the knowledge that he wants what's best for him. But that's just not the reality of our situation.

To: Ethan
From: Mum
Not this time, bud. I won't let him. And don't be sorry, it's not your fault. I'll see you later.

"Everything okay?" Brody's velvet voice asks.

I glance up and feel calmer at just the sight of him. As much as I hate that he had to shake hands with Chad, and as worried as I was about him finding out the public status of Ethan's dad – I'm glad he was here next to me. I'm not sure what would have happened if he wasn't.

"I've told you; you *have* to stop asking if I'm okay," I tease, trying to lighten the mood.

"No deal today, Morgs," he replies simply, his voice tight, but his eyes soft. "You ready to get out of here?" he asks.

I nod.

I've never been more ready; I've felt on edge ever since Chad left – part of me thinks he's still lurking around somewhere waiting to get me alone.

He turns to his friend and sister. "Well, it's been... *an experience...* we're out – see you guys later."

Adam waves, his mouth somehow still full. Olivia scowls at her brother and gives me a smile. "See you soon, Morgan."

"Sure will," I reply.

I like Olivia. She's cool. I haven't got many friends, but I wouldn't mind having a friend like Olivia. She says what she thinks, and it doesn't seem like she plays games – other than trying to make Adam mad.

Brody's arm comes around me and lands on my shoulders. He's tall enough that I'm the perfect height for him to rest there comfortably.

I love the way he can rest his chin on the top of my head.

Chad used to be able to do that when we were young.

I really have always had a thing for tall guys. He's not as tall as Brody, not even close, but he's tall enough.

Brody walks me out of the café and glances around, looking to see that Chad isn't out here somewhere I assume.

He swings open the passenger door and helps me into my seat. He lingers for a moment, his eyes trained on mine before he presses a soft kiss to my lips and steps back, closing the door.

My heart races, the same way it did when Chad kissed my cheek – but for entirely different reasons.

Chad makes me anxious; Brody makes me excited.

I watch as he climbs in, starts the engine and drives us away.

I don't say anything as he turns off to the beach and parks up in the carpark overlooking the sea.

He turns off the engine, undoes his belt and twists in his seat to look at me.

"So... your ex is football legend, Chad Jenson."

I nod nervously. "He's no legend in my eyes, but yeah... the one and only..."

He nods slowly, processing.

"Ethan told him I was seeing someone," I say before he can ask, because it's obvious he wants answers. "He said he mentioned it by accident – we were out together when Chad called."

He narrows his eyes slightly. "You say that like you didn't want Chad to find out..."

I shrug. "I don't like him in my business." It's not a lie, but it's not the whole truth. I didn't want Chad to know about Brody because he'll scare him off.

"You think that's why he's turned up here, don't you?" he asks softly.

I shrug again. "Maybe. He was probably due to show up sometime this year, but the timing is... *interesting*."

I stare out the window and think about the fact that he's shown up here and now – no doubt on a mission to mess things up for me again.

"He's done that before?"

I nod, my eyes drifting back to meet his. "A couple of times... I never told him anything much about my life, but when we still lived back home, he always found out everything I did... who I went out with... his old buddies kept an eye on me and who I spent time with. That's the main reason we moved out here. To get some space."

"How long ago did you move?"

"Five years, it was the best move I ever made. He hasn't interfered in my business since we moved... there's no real reason that he'd be here to do that now... but..."

"But it feels like he is, right?"

He thrums his fingers against the steering wheel. "Have the two of you ever tried to make it work again, you know, when you were older?"

That's the question I was hoping he wouldn't ask. It's the one that will make me look like a silly naïve little girl when I answer it.

"There's been a couple of... attempts," I reply vaguely, even though I know he won't leave it at that.

"He messed you around, didn't he?"

I half nod, half shrug. "There was one time, Ethan was about six – Chad had been away for the entire football season. He hadn't seen Ethan for months and months, and he called one day out of the blue... *anyway*, Ethan told him that Dave –

a guy I was seeing at the time – had taken us to the fair... Chad lost the plot. He came home when he should have been with the team, he got rid of Dave and told me he wanted me back."

"So, you took him back."

"He told me everything I'd ever wanted to hear from him."

It still hurts now, not that he screwed me over, but that I was stupid enough to let him.

"It lasted about two weeks. He went back to the team, partied hard, made the headlines with some bimbo in his lap, and I went back into the shadows to lick my wounds."

I never let him into my heart again. I wish I could say the same about my bed.

"What an asshole." He grips the steering wheel tightly, his knuckles turning white. "The way he looked at you today, Morgs... I didn't like it."

I didn't like it either – even though it was probably only for Brody's benefit.

The way he looked at me made me nervous.

He looked like he wanted me again.

I always told myself I was using him the same way he was using me, but it never felt like that when he left.

"That's the way he always looks at me. That's what he does."

"He looked like he wanted to fuck you," he replies harshly, and I feel my face heat.

I pop a shoulder, but don't say anything.

He runs a hand over his face. "Please tell me that you don't let that asshole have you like that?" He's asking me a tough question, but I don't feel judgement from him. He's frustrated, yes, but he's not judging me.

"Not anymore."

He reaches over and takes my hand in his. "Morgs... you deserve so much better than that, than *him*."

"I know."

Only, I'm not sure I do know. I did let him waltz in and out of my life for over ten years after all.

"When was the last time?"

"Before we left town. We've only seen him a few times since we moved out here, and they've been flying visits."

"Do you still love him?"

I shake my head. "No. I'm not sure I ever did. I think I could have, if he'd shown up for us... if he'd been the kind of man we deserved... I think that's all I was ever hoping for, you know? That one day he'd come to his senses and we could be a real family."

"Do you still wish for that?" Brody asks, and I don't miss the hint of hurt in his voice.

"Do I wish that the father of my child would step up and be a dad? Hell yes – Ethan could use a real dad... do I want him to be with me...." I shake my head, "no, not anymore."

His fingers wrap around mine a little tighter. "This is a lot to take in."

That's an understatement. I wouldn't blame him for running a mile right now.

"I know, and I know it's not what you thought you were getting yourself into when you asked for my number that night. You didn't know I came with a kid and a dodgy ex. I won't blame you if you need some time to process... I won't even blame you if you decide it's all too much."

"Morgs, I—"

"Don't," I cut him off. "I don't expect you to answer me about it now. Take some time. Think it through."

He looks conflicted, but he nods.

"In fact," I glance out at the crashing waves, "I might go for a walk – I can get a cab home, so you don't have to wait."

"I can drive you home."

I shake my head. "I'm a big girl, Brody." I lean across and kiss his cheek. "Take some time. I'll do the same. A bit of space might do some good."

He doesn't reply, but nods once.

I smile tightly at him and open the car door.

Tears prick at my eyes – this feels like goodbye. I don't want it to be, but that's how it feels. Maybe Chad has succeeded without even trying this time.

CHAPTER THIRTEEN

Brody

"Should I have gone after her?"

"I don't think you really need me to answer that question," Olivia says, an unimpressed expression on her face.

I've just spilled my guts, telling her everything about Morgan and the situation with her ex.

"She said she wanted some space to think," I argue.

"That's girl code for 'fight for me.'"

"That makes no sense."

"Tell me about it." She shrugs. "But that's how it is; we virtually never say what we mean."

"Why the hell not?" I demand.

She crosses her arms across her chest. "Now is not the time to try and figure out the world's best kept secrets, B, now is the time to decide if you want the woman or not."

"Of course, I want her. I never stopped wanting her."

"Did you tell her that?"

"Not *exactly*."

"Idiot," she replies with a shake of her head.

I cross my arms, mimicking her position. "So, I'm expected to speak secret women language, but also say exactly how I feel in simple English without any hidden meanings?"

She groans. "Of *course,* you are! She's the vulnerable one in this situation, not *you*. It sounds like she's been dealing with a mind fuck of an ex since she was just a kid herself, and then you come along, waltzing into her life like a breath of fresh air... Do you really think that she expects anything other than for it all to turn to shit?"

I hadn't thought about it like that.

Morgan is used to being let down... used.

But I'm not that guy.

"What about her ex? He's here to cause trouble, I can tell," I grumble.

"So, let him try. If you're being a good man, then there's nothing he can do to hurt you."

I can think of plenty he could do to hurt me, all of which involve hurting Morgan, but I try not to think about that.

"Does he bother you that much?" she asks.

I nod. "He bothers me a whole fucking lot, and not because he's her ex, but because he messes with her head, and because he's a shitty dad. Ethan deserves better – they both do."

"So, go be that better for them," she says simply.

I huff out a laugh. She's right. It's just as easy as that.

I can be better, fuck it, I *am* better than him. I can treat Morgan the way she deserves to be treated.

"I can tell you care about this woman, so if you don't do something about it, I might hit you," she threatens.

"You think I've fucked it up beyond repair?"

She laughs. "Don't be stupid. She's given you an easy out here – now she's just waiting to see if you take it or not."

"I don't want an easy out."

"You're telling the wrong girl."

Of course, I am.

"Right. Good chat, Liv, thanks."

"No problem, you big dummy."

I head out the door immediately. There is somewhere else I need to be.

"Oh, and just so you know… you are *so* screwed!" she calls after me, and I shake my head with a chuckle.

I *am* so screwed, and I'm completely good with it.

***

I pull up outside her place and jog up the path to her front door. I rap my knuckles against the door, but there's no answer.

I glance at the screen on my phone, there's no reply to the text I sent on my way over here either.

I knock again, but the inside of the house is dead silent.

I left her at the beach over two hours ago, surely she should be back by now.

My mind races, imagining her ex following her to the beach and talking to her alone.

I don't know if my blood runs cold because I'm worried he might hurt her, or because he might convince her that it's a good idea for the two of them to try again.

I sit down on the front step and drop my face into my hands.

I pull my phone out again and try to call her. She still doesn't answer.

I stretch out my legs in front of me, settling in. I'm not leaving until either I see her, or she calls me back, I decide.

Olivia is always calling me stubborn; I think it's about time I started acting like it.

This is going to go one of two ways, and I'll be damned if I go before I find out which of the two it is.

I sit for half an hour before I hear her voice.

I get to my feet and glance down the street. She's strolling along, her shoes in her hands, her feet still with sand on them.

She must have walked all the way from the beach.

She's talking on the phone, and the look on her face puts me on edge.

I was going to stand here and wait, but the expression she's sporting won't allow me to stay put.

I stride down the path, pushing her front gate further open and jog down the footpath until I'm standing right in front of her.

Her eyes widen and she stops walking as she watches me approach.

"Thank you, officer, yes I'll be sure to let you know if I hear or see anything."

I frown as I listen to her side of the conversation.

I don't know why the hell she's talking to a police officer, but whatever it's about, I don't like it.

My eyes rake over her quickly from head to toe, looking for any sign that there's a hair out of place. If someone has touched her, I'll kill them.

There's nothing though, she looks perfect.

"It's okay, it's not your fault. Thanks for letting me know – I'll call you if I notice anything else. Bye."

She brings the phone down from her ear, her expression a mix of shock and confusion.

"What's wrong, Morgs?"

My hands find her shoulders and hold her.

She frowns at me. "You're here?"

I grin. "Of course, I'm here. You didn't think I was going to give up that easily, did you?"

Her top teeth sink into her soft bottom lip, the corners of her mouth curling up into a sweet smile.

She presses forward, her arms wrapping around my waist, the side of her face pressing against my chest. She releases a deep breath that seems a lot like relief.

I sigh and breathe in deeply, the scent of her shampoo overtaking everything else.

"I'm so glad you're here," she says softly.

I pry her hands from my middle and bring her out in front of me so I can look her in the eye. I haven't forgotten my question.

"Why were you talking to the cops?"

"They had to release him... the creep from the bar," she whispers.

"What?" I reply harshly, "what the fuck did they do that for?"

"His lawyer found some missing paperwork... got him out on bail until the police can get everything in order. They're still hoping to get a conviction, but it's going to take a little bit of time."

I don't like this. Not at all. That prick could have gotten Morgan's name by now – from there it wouldn't take much to find her. She's got a huge fucking sign out the front of her place with her phone number on it for crying out loud.

"For fuck's sake, so he's just out there, wandering around looking for his next victim? He could come after you."

She shrugs. "I'm sure it'll be okay."

She's not convincing me in the slightest.

My minds races and her conversation echoes in my ears.

"Hang on a minute, you said 'I'll call you if I notice any-thing else', what the hell does that mean, Morgs?" I demand, dipping my head so we're face to face.

She tries to avoid my gaze but I'm not having it.

"*Morgan*," I warn.

"I thought I saw a car following me the other day – a white one. Then I swear I saw it parked outside the house this morning. It's nothing, Brody, honestly... I'm just paranoid... but when they called today to tell me he had been out a few days, I thought it couldn't hurt to pass along the info about the car."

"Someone *followed* you and you didn't tell me?"

She shrugs. "I don't think they were really following me, like I said, I'm paranoid."

Fuck that. Morgan is no fool, and if she has reason to be-lieve that she was being followed, then I believe it too.

"If you see *anything* that makes you feel even the littlest bit uncomfortable, I want you to call me, right away, okay?"

"Does that mean you're hanging around?"

I reach for her face, cupping it in my hand as I wrap my oth-er hand around her middle to drag her against me.

I crush my lips to hers, my mouth owning her.

There's no way I'm going anywhere.

She pulls away, her breath coming in heavy pants.

"I guess that answers that question," she whispers, her fin-gers gripping my shirt.

"Promise me, Morgan," I rasp.

"I promise," she breathes before kissing me again.

CHAPTER FOURTEEN

Brody

"Ethan is going to stay over at Lachie's tonight," Morgan tells me as she appears on her front step, a glass of cold water in her hand that she offers to me.

I take it from her and down the whole thing in one go.

I've spent the past thirty minutes removing the sign from her front yard – she didn't think it was necessary, but I didn't agree. Not at fucking all.

It can go up outside my place, or the gym or anywhere that isn't here. Somewhere where there are security cameras to get past and me to deal with.

"Good. So, you're free for the night then?"

I chuckle when I see the look on her face.

Her eyes are trained on my chest, her lip tugged into her mouth. I don't even think she heard me speak.

It got hot out here, I *had* to take my shirt off. It was like I didn't even have a choice.

"My face is up here, Morgs."

"But your abs are down there," she says with a laugh.

Can't argue with that. I like her eyes on me anyway. It's good for my self-esteem.

"You didn't answer me?"

"Huh?" She tips her head to the side, her eyes finally meeting mine. "Oh yeah, I'm free as a bird, probably do something exciting like order a pizza and watch a movie."

"Sounds perfect."

She arches a brow. "You stooping to inviting yourself over now, slick?"

"Nope." I shake my head. "You're coming to my place where I know you're safe."

She rolls her eyes. "Oh *c'mon*, I told you I was overreacting. It was probably just a neighbour's car parked on the street or something totally innocent like that."

"I don't give a shit," I reply simply. "You're coming with me, even if I have to drag you there kicking and screaming."

I wouldn't really, but given the sexy smirk on her face, I'm sure it won't come to that anyway. She wants to come with me, I know she does.

"You're awfully bossy."

When it comes to her and her safety, fuck yes, I am. I already care too much about her.

I shrug. "I've had a hell of a day, Morgs – between meeting your asshole ex, thinking I was losing you and then finding out a creep that drugged you may or may not be stalking you, I'm about ready to throw you over my shoulder and handcuff you to something solid."

"Well," she grins, "why didn't you start with the handcuffs?"

I chuckle and wipe the sweat from my brow on the back of my hand.

Her gaze drifts back to my torso. "You *really* are giving my neighbours a treat today."

"I'm only really interested in giving *you* a treat." I growl as I stand at full height and cross my arms across my chest.

She gasps and I chuckle.

"I'll go pack a bag then," she says.

***

"You miss the game, slick?"

I smile as I take her in. She's lying on my couch, her feet in my lap as we watch one of my all-time favourite movies, *Coach Carter*. I'm such a cliché basketball guy – at least that's what Morgan tells me.

She looks so relaxed, like she doesn't have a care in the world. She looks as though she feels safe, which is no small feat given the things today has thrown at her.

"Yeah, I miss it. It's not so bad since I still get to coach, but I miss hanging out with guys my own age – I miss that team spirit."

"So why don't you coach the main team?"

I huff out a laugh. "They're the top team in the country, Morgs, I doubt they'd be interested in even hearing me out."

She shakes her head at me, her eyes shining like she's privy to some secret I'm not. "You just wait, I bet you'll get there – if that's what you want, you'll get there, slick."

I've never really thought much about it. I'd love to coach the pro players. I would, but after my injury, I haven't had time to dream too big. I had to deal with my career being over, and then I had to adjust to being the coach of the next generation of basketball.

It's not that I don't like working with the youth team, because I do – but coaching the pros would be a whole other ball game – excuse the pun – it would be a challenge, and I'm sure the time will come when I want a challenge that size again.

"I guess we'll see," I reply as I tickle her feet.

She shrieks and throws her legs off me. "Oh my god, *don't* touch my feet, they're so ticklish!"

I grin wickedly and she backs up as far as she can, until the arm of the couch is pressed against her back. She hurriedly tucks her feet underneath her body.

"*Brody*," she warns as I prowl closer. "No!" she cries, a huge grin on her face as I grab hold of one of her thighs and drag her back towards me.

"Are you ticklish anywhere else?" I taunt her as I run my other hand up her side.

She shakes her head furiously, but she's lying, I can tell.

I slide my fingers under her top and lightly drag them over the exposed skin I find there. She writhes below me, a laugh bursting out of her.

Her hands are grabbing at mine as she tries to escape.

"Stop!" she giggles, "I might pee myself."

I chuckle and rest my hand on her rib cage, my fingers stilling.

She relaxes after a few beats and wipes at the tears in her eyes. "You're a monster." She grins.

"Sure am, baby."

I slide my hand further up her jeans-clad thigh, and she watches the movement with an intensity that wasn't there a moment ago.

She's willing me to keep going, so I do, the hand under her shirt sliding around and over her bra. I can feel the lace under my fingers, and it makes me want to rip the shirt from her body so I can see it for myself.

"You've had that shirt off half the day, what's it still doing on now?" she murmurs.

She makes a good point.

I reluctantly pull my hands from her body and lift the hem of my shirt over my head before discarding it on the floor beside the couch.

She sits up, her hands already roaming over the parts of me she was studying so closely earlier.

I sit back, my legs wide and tug on her until she climbs into my lap.

She brings her face to mine, her warm breath fanning my face. I press my lips to hers, and what starts out as a slow, lingering kiss, quickly turns into something far hotter and heavier.

Her nails dig into the skin on my shoulders and I welcome the sharp pain.

I grip her ass and lift her so she's closer, pressed against me and sitting on my dick that is now undeniably hard inside my jeans.

She reaches for the hem of her top and begins to lift it over her head, revealing a strip of the creamy-coloured skin on her stomach.

"Are you sure about this, Morgs?" I ask, my voice husky.

I want her to be sure, damn sure, because I know exactly where this is heading – with me inside her.

She smiles wickedly and pulls her top the rest of the way off.

"You're about the only thing I feel truly sure of today," she whispers as she clasps my jaw in her hands.

My hands splay across her back and I feel her skin break out into goosebumps.

"I just want everything to be perfect for you," I whisper back.

She laughs softly. "I don't need perfect, but you know what? You're as close as I've ever seen."

She leans in and just when I think she's going to kiss me, she nips at my bottom lip, tugging it into her mouth.

I growl deep in my throat, and I'm on my feet in as instant, her in my arms.

She gasps, her legs wrapping around my waist and holding on tight.

I stride across the room and press her against the wall with a thud, my mouth slanting down on hers, rough and possessive.

"I've wanted you since the moment I laid eyes on you," I growl. "I couldn't take my eyes off you in that bar. It was embarrassing."

My lips graze over the skin on her throat, and she rolls her head back, moaning.

"So... I wasn't... just some damsel in... distress to you?" she asks, her words coming out in short, sharp, pants.

"Not even close," I growl, "ask Liv, I couldn't focus on anything but you."

I've got her hands pinned above her head, the pressure of my body against hers is the only thing stopping her from sliding down the wall.

"Take me to bed, Coach Owens," she whispers.

I chuckle; I plan to do exactly that. My hands release hers so she can hold on to me as I carry her up the flight of stairs that lead to my bedroom.

Her face is buried in my neck, her arms wrapped around my neck and shoulders, and I can't even recall a time where I felt this content.

Basketball fulfilled me, but not like this.

Being with women has never been a bad thing, but it's never been this intense – all consuming.

I know that already, even this early on, I'd do *anything* for this woman.

I stop before my bed and unhook her legs from my hips so she can stand on the ground.

I have to hunch my shoulders and dip my head to get our faces level, but I don't care. I'll deal with a crook neck if it means I get to kiss her any time I like.

I kiss her once, softly before taking a step back so I can really look at her.

I don't want to miss a second of what's about to happen.

She stares at me for a few beats with those pretty green eyes, her gaze lingering longer on my chest than anywhere else.

I undo the button on my jeans and slide down my fly; I've never been so eager to be rid of a pair of pants in my life.

I tug them down my long legs and stomp them to the ground.

"You're just so tall." She sighs, her voice dreamy.

I laugh. I certainly am.

"Tall does it for you, huh, Morgs?"

She nods her head slowly. "Sure does."

She does it for me too, but right now, she's wearing far too much clothing.

She must feel the same way because she starts stripping off her own jeans, and before I can say 'holy shit' she's standing before me in only her white lace bra and a black thong.

That's it. That's my limit, the most I can take.

I've got her pressed against the mattress two seconds after my eyes land on her, and I've got my boxer briefs on the floor only a few seconds after that.

Her bra follows and her thong is right behind it.

I don't care how good they look on her body, they look infinitely better off.

We don't say a word to one another. Not as she reaches down to stroke my hard length, or as I work my fingers in and out of her until she writhes.

The only sounds as I sheath myself with a condom and push deep inside of her are her soft moans of pleasure.

CHAPTER FIFTEEN

Morgan

It's days like these that I wish I had at least one good girlfriend, so I could call her and tell her about the spine-tingling, toe-curling sex I've been having.

I'd tell her *everything* about Brody.

I'd tell her how safe he makes me feel – how *protected*. I'd tell her about how his touch sets me on fire and how I'm falling in love with him.

I'd tell her how completely consumed I am with him.

I don't think about anything else while I'm with Brody, not about Chad, not about the creep from the bar – not even about my son.

I only think about him, *us*.

Now, that might not be the first paragraph in the 'how to be a good parent' guide, but I figure after sixteen years old being a dedicated single parent, I'm owed a few nights of being selfish.

I grin as I toss my phone into my handbag.

Brody text me earlier and it was just three words, 'Come back already'. He sent it thirty seconds after he finally let me leave. I've read it about fifty times since.

I had to run out on him earlier; I had to work this afternoon, and I knew he had to go to practice anyway.

I have to go and pick up Ethan when it's over.

I giggle to myself as I think about what an absolute chore it will be to see his sexy coach again.

I glance in my rear-view mirror several times as I drive across town to make sure no one is following, something that is apparently a habit for me now.

No matter what I tell Brody about relaxing, I can't seem to truly relax when I'm alone.

I told him that the white car was nothing, but the more I think about it, the more it becomes *something*.

I've had two more phone calls where no one was there when I answered too.

Brody seems to have forgotten about that happening the other day when he answered my phone, and I'm not about to remind him either.

I love how protective of me he seems to be, but I don't need him any more on edge than he already is.

I thought for a minute there that he was going to insist on coming to work with me this afternoon. If it weren't for the fact that my assistant was going to be there, I think he would have.

I turn off towards the gym and a white car pulling in behind me catches my attention.

My heart pounds as it turns off the main highway behind me.

I press the accelerator a little heavier into the ground, but the car keeps pace with me. It's flashy and expensive-looking, the silver horse on the front grill is shining at me like a beacon.

I can't make out the driver through the heavy tints, but I'm about to panic and call the officer who gave me his direct line when the car turns off, leaving me with a racing pulse and a feeling of stupidity.

I need to calm down.

I'm being stupid. There are about five million white cars around, and I don't even know if the man who tried to drug me drives one or not.

There is no reason for me to believe that this guy would come after me.

I'm fine. I'm fine. I'm fine.

If I say it enough times, maybe I'll start believing it.

I need to give myself a pep talk.

The white car I think I keep seeing is nothing more than a coincidence. I know nothing about cars – I doubt I'd be able to recognise if the car I saw each time was the same or different, and the calls with no answer are probably nothing more than a dodgy phone line from someone who's trying to view or list a property.

I need to make myself believe that the man who tried to drug me isn't coming after me, because I can't expect Brody to be at my side twenty-four seven to calm me down, and right now, that's all I can think about... getting to him and breathing him in.

I'm coming to rely on him far too much, I'm falling for him too quickly, but how could I not? He's gorgeous, kind, caring and he looks at me like I'm something special... he's not put off by the fact that I have a teenager at home, and he makes me feel like my heart is going to leap out of my chest with nothing more than a smile.

I pull into the carpark, shut off my engine and hurriedly rush into the building. Practice still has half an hour to go, so there are hardly any cars in the carpark, but I'm not willing to wait out here for Ethan – I'm shaken now.

I cross the carpark and almost jog into the foyer, my heels clicking against the hard floor.

I let out a deep breath at the sight of him.

He's wearing his signature baseball cap on his head, and his long, defined muscles look familiar and comforting.

He hasn't even seen me yet, but I instantly feel at ease.

I'm being silly.

I'm fine. No one is following me. I haven't inherited a stalker.

This time I believe it. I can reason with myself when Brody is near.

I don't know how long I stand there silently watching him interact with the boys, but when I hear a noise behind me, it startles me only a little bit, rather than making me jump out of my skin like it would have when I first arrived.

Practice is nearly over, and some of the parents are probably turning up to collect their kids.

I smile to myself as I think about talking to the mums about Brody – I know I shouldn't... they already look at him like a piece of meat, I should *definitely* not share his sex life with them, but that doesn't stop me from wanting to brag about him anyway.

I really do miss girl talk.

I stroll away from the window to see who's arrived.

I glance once more over my shoulder, and I see Brody looking in my direction, he's not looking at me though, he's frowning at something over my shoulder.

I take another step and collide with someone.

"Sorry, I..." The words are out of my mouth before I see who I've crashed into.

Chad looks down at me, his hands on my shoulders and a smile on his face.

"What are you doing here?" I ask, my voice surprised.

"Same as you. I came to watch Ethan."

I've spent more time watching my son's coach than I have actually watching him, but I'm not about to tell Chad that.

I also don't like that he's here. I can't say I'm totally shocked – after his inappropriate comments at the café, I didn't think I would get away that easily, but I don't like him being here. He's never been supportive of Ethan playing basketball, but there's nothing I can do about it. He's got as much right to be here as I do. I just have to wait this out – hope that he'll get bored like he usually does and disappear back to his real life – wherever and whatever that might involve.

The difference between now and then though, is Brody. I know that, and so does Chad.

He's like a spoiled child that wants all the toys for himself even when he's not playing with them.

He doesn't want me, or his son, not when it really comes down to it, but he doesn't want anybody else to have us either.

He's a narcissist. Always has been, always will be.

"Can't you just go back home?" I ask, an edge of begging to my voice.

He smirks arrogantly. "Oh, c'mon, princess, I just got into town, you want me to leave already?"

I huff out a laugh. "Yes. I do. Is that so hard to believe?" I shrug off his hands, and step backwards, but he steps with me.

"I don't think you really want me to leave, Morgan... I think *he* wants me to." He tips his head over my shoulder, and I know he's referring to Brody.

I don't look, because that's what Chad wants me to do. Instead I cross my arms across my chest and try to remember how to be the confident, self-assured woman I am when Brody is around.

I need to channel her big time right now.

"What makes you think I want you to stay?"

His blue eyes sparkle, and I get the distinct impression I've just walked into a trap of some sort.

"Same thing that made me stay years ago... we used to have fun, Morgan... we could have fun again."

Yeah, it was real *fun* when he slept with me, let me believe we could really have something, and then rode off into the sunset.

That was *so much* fun for me.

"I've got someone else to have fun with now."

His eyes narrow and harden, and I know I've really pissed him off with that statement.

I don't know why – he's never laid a finger on me – but when he looks at me with that feral look in his eyes, I feel intimidated.

"You think that prick can give you what I can?"

"What?" I demand, finding strength from some place inside me that I didn't know existed. "A shitty relationship and a non-existent father figure? You really set the bar high."

His eyes are still dark and intense, so I take another step backwards, and this time he doesn't follow.

He stares at me hard for a long moment and then his expression softens, and he grins wide at me.

I hate how handsome he looks when he smiles.

"I can be better than that, Morgan, I want to be better. I want my family back."

If I had a dollar for every time I'd heard that, well… I'd probably only have about fifty bucks, but still. This isn't new, and as per usual, it's nothing but total shit.

I thought we'd moved on from this when Ethan and I moved away, but it's becoming apparent to me now that his sudden reappearance has more to do with the fact that I've moved on than it does with him suddenly wanting to be a dad or boyfriend.

"I'm not interested, Chad."

"Are you sure?" He presses, stepping towards me again.

I back up a few steps but there's nowhere for me to go now, not without turning and running like a scared little girl, and I won't give him the satisfaction.

"Are you *really* sure, Morgan? I see the way you still look at me."

I hate that he knows how attractive he his, but even given how easy he is on the eye, I feel *nothing* for him. There's no attraction, no connection – he's just some guy who donated me some sperm once.

I hear the thundering of feet and see over his shoulder that the entire team has just sprinted through the foyer and out the front door – Brody has sent them to run a lap of the outside of the gym.

"Just save your efforts for Ethan, I don't need you, never have, never will," I say.

Chad goes to take another step towards me, but stops dead in his tracks, his eyes leaving my face and drifting over my shoulder.

I feel him before I hear or see him.

His arm snakes around me protectively, his chin coming to rest on the top of my head.

I sigh in relief.

I don't want to be here having this awkward conversation with my prick of an ex – I want to be thinking about my future, one that will hopefully involve Brody.

"Chad," Brody says, his voice tight.

"Coach Owens," Chad replies arrogantly, his hands sliding casually into his suit pants pockets.

He might be an absolute ass, but he wears the shit out of a suit.

Brody lowers his mouth to my ear. "You alright, baby?" he whispers for only me to hear.

I nod.

I was fine, but I'm better now.

Both of my hands clasp Brody's hand that has settled around my middle.

"Chad was just trying to take a walk down memory lane."

"I bet he was," Brody mutters.

Chad's eyes narrow, but they're not focused on me anymore, that look is directed at Brody.

I hate the way he's shooting daggers, but Brody doesn't seem bothered as he kisses the top of my head.

"Morgs, do you mind going into the gym and talking to Steve a minute? Ethan rolled his ankle earlier and Steve just wants to run through a couple of exercises with you."

I glance up at him, but his dark eyes are looking at my ex, not at me.

It's clear they're about to have words, and that Brody wants to do it alone.

I nod my head and nibble on my bottom lip nervously.

I step away, but at the last second, Brody tugs me back, spinning me so our chests collide, before bringing his lips down to meet mine.

I gasp at the intensity of the kiss.

I know what he's doing. He's staking his claim. He's showing Chad that I'm his. It might be stupid and caveman-like, but I don't care.

I walk away in a daze, my gaze not even once flitting to the man who broke my heart.

CHAPTER SIXTEEN

Brody

We're going to have a little chat, this douche and me.

A chat and nothing more – as much as I'd love to come out swinging, I'm not stupid enough to put my hands on a super star – not out here in public where anyone could see anyway.

I'd be slapped with a lawsuit faster than I could say 'ex-boyfriend'.

Arrogance surrounds him, like a little bubble he likes to live in.

I cross my arms firmly across my chest. He mimics me, and we stand there in a silent standoff.

I'm taller than him, but he's broader.

"How long are you in town?" I finally ask, when it's obvious he's waiting for me to speak.

"As long as it takes."

I arch a brow, but don't ask the question he's trying to goad me into asking.

"You know, she's never going to settle down with you. She hasn't had anything serious in the past sixteen years," he says when I don't reply.

"No, I bet you saw to that."

He smirks, confirming Morgan's suspicions that he *does* step in and interferes with her life whenever he feels like it.

"You'll have to try harder if you're going to get rid of me."

He nods, his expression thoughtful. "I've always liked a challenge."

I chuckle darkly. It'll be a challenge alright. There's nothing he could say or do that would change the fact that I've fallen in love with the mother of his child.

"Have you even seen Ethan since you got here?" I ask; it's a dig at him, but it's also a curious question. I really can't tell if he gives a shit about his son or not.

"I'm here, aren't I?"

I go to say something more, but I'm cut off by the sound of the boys pouring back into the building.

"Nice work today, boys," I call out to them as I point into the gym, "go and stretch out, and I'll see you in a couple of days."

They nod their heads, a chorus of 'thanks Coach' coming at me as they file through the doors, most of them breathing hard from the exertion.

"Dad?" I hear Ethan ask. His voice sounds surprised.

He pushes through the line and glances at his father warily. "What are you doing here?"

Chad plasters on a bright smile and claps his hand on Ethan's back.

"Came to see if my son was ready to ditch this game yet and come join his father on a football field."

Ethan shrugs, and I don't miss the way he slides away a fraction, so that Chad's hand drops.

He doesn't know what to say, I can tell this isn't the first time Chad has made this 'joke'.

"Head into the gym and finish up, Eth, I'll be there in a minute to go over that play with you."

Ethan nods gratefully at me. "Thanks, Coach." He grins.

I nod my head once at him.

Chad scowls, his lip twitching with obvious irritation.

"Ethan is one of my best players," I tell him.

It's the truth, but even if it wasn't, I like the way I can talk about Ethan to his so-called dad. I think I know more about the kid than he does.

Chad is getting more and more pissed off by the second, and I'm starting to enjoy myself.

"Yeah?" he growls. "That have anything to do with the fact that you're fucking his mum?"

I huff out a humourless laugh and take a step in his direction.

"First thing – I'm *dating* her, not just fucking her – and I'd be doing it even if he sucked at playing ball."

He growls and I chuckle.

"You'll steer clear of my family if you know what's good for you," he threatens, and I have to really work hard to not grab him by his shirt and slam him into a wall.

They're not his family.

Getting a woman pregnant doesn't make her yours, and fathering a child doesn't make you a dad.

"This is what we do, the three of us. They're always there when I want them, and I'm not about to let some retired basketball player change that."

I glance through the viewing window into the main stadium and find Morgan watching the two of us carefully. Ethan is shooting hoops, and casting glances between his mum and us every few seconds.

They both deserve so much better than this loser.

"Are you trying to scare me off?" I ask as I turn my attention back to him.

"Maybe, is it working?"

"Do I look scared?" I drawl.

He doesn't say another word. He shoots me a look of displeasure, turns on his heel, and then he's gone.

***

I take the key from her and insert it in the lock. "I'm telling you, Morgs, I didn't give you a chance to say no."

Ethan bounces his basketball and grins at me. "He's right, Mum, you can't say no when he didn't ask a question."

I point at him. "He's a smart kid."

Ethan leaves us in the entry, bounding off into the house.

I close the door behind us and lock it again.

"We don't need babysitting; I swear we'll be fine."

"I know you will." I come up behind her as she hangs her coat on the hook by the door and wrap my arms around her middle, my chin resting on her shoulder. "This has nothing to do with creepy men and everything to do with me being completely and utterly obsessed with spending every free minute I have with you."

She sighs heavily and wiggles around, so her front is pressed against mine.

She reaches up, draping her arms around my neck. "Well... when you say it like that..."

I search her green eyes, there's something bothering her, I can tell. "What is it?"

She shakes her head, but when she stills, I'm still there, staring, seeing more than she might want to share.

"Morgan."

She sighs again. "I saw a white car in my mirror today and I panicked. It was nothing, just a random white car and I was this close to having a meltdown." She holds her finger and thumb a few millimetres apart. "Maybe I'm not as tough as I like to think I am."

I hate that she's feeling like this. I wish I could be there twenty-four seven to protect her and make her feel safe, but the reality is, I can't.

I glance around to see if Ethan is anywhere eavesdropping, but there's no sign of him.

"I'm going to call the cops, have them find out if this guy even drives a white car," I announce, letting go of her and taking her hand so I can drag her into the living room.

I pull her into my lap as I sit on the couch and she snuggles in gratefully.

I slide my phone out of my pocket and start searching for the number.

"There's something else," she mutters, so quietly, I almost don't hear it.

"What?" I reply quickly, my heart rate speeding up.

"It's probably just some kids, or someone with a bad line, but you remember the other day when you answered my phone and then no one was there when I got on the phone?"

I nod.

"Well it's happened a couple more times."

"Give me the number," I demand.

"Private line," she whispers.

"Shit." I run my hand through my hair in frustration and she curls up tighter, making herself smaller.

"I'm scared," she admits.

My arms come around her in an instant, comforting her, rubbing slow circles on her back.

"You should have told me. How can I keep you safe if I don't know what's going on?"

"Honestly, I feel pathetic. Nothing has even happened to me."

"You've got every right to be sc–"

I'm cut off by her phone ringing from her bag on the couch next to us.

I grab it, my arms are longer than hers, and hand it to her.

She pulls it out of her bag, glances at it and then tosses it onto the couch with a groan.

"It's Chad."

I inhale through my nose. I'm running out of patience with this guy.

I reach for the phone.

"Just ignore him," she whispers.

The phone stops ringing, but promptly starts up again.

Fuck this. I'm not going to sit here listening to a ringing phone all night. I want to enjoy this time with my girl.

"Hello?" I answer.

I hear a displeased click of his tongue and then he responds. "Is Morgan there?"

"Nope," I reply simply.

"Look, Owens, I need to speak to her."

"I'll be happy to pass on a message."

He makes a noise of irritation and it occurs to me then that he's a man used to getting exactly what he wants. He's the famous rich guy who nobody ever says no to.

Unfortunately for him, that's not going to fly around here.

I don't give a fuck who he is in the football world. In my world, he's just a pain in the ass.

"You're barking up the wrong fucking tree here—"

I chuckle and hang up the phone before he can even finish his threat.

I glance down at Morgan and she's grinning. "He's mad."

"He's really fucking mad," I amend.

"He won't just let this slide."

I shrug. "I'm not scared of him, Morgs, and you don't have to be either, not anymore. He can't do anything to you – not on my watch."

Her eyes soften. "Should I be falling for you this fast?" she asks in a whisper.

I trace the curve of her cheek with my finger, my heart thumping against my rib cage.

"Definitely," I reply quietly.

"Good, because you sure know how to sweep a woman off her feet."

"It's one of my skills," I whisper back.

She giggles softly.

I bring my mouth to her ear. "You're really falling for me, Morgs?"

She nods, slowly but surely, my mouth inching towards hers.

"Good, because you're taking me down with you."

"You two are so gross." Ethan's voice comes from the doorway, killing the moment.

Morgan tries to pull away, but I hold her close.

"You wanna go away a minute, man?" I ask Ethan without so much as glancing at him.

"Not particularly," he says, his tone cocky.

"Well you might want to shut your eyes then."

I press my lips to Morgan's and hear Ethan groan and his footsteps retreating back up the hall.

I did try to warn him.

Morgan giggles against my lips. "Poor kid."

"He'll live." I chuckle. "I've heard what they talk about in the gym – a kiss is nothing."

"I do not want to know." She shudders.

"I think it's best you don't," I reply with a grin.

CHAPTER SEVENTEEN

Morgan

"I've got bad news, baby…" Brody's voice fills my car as I drive towards an open home I'm hosting in about an hour's time.

"Real bad news? Or like the other night when you text me to tell me you had bad news and it was just that you'd run out of peanut butter?" I grin.

He huffs out a laugh but there's no real humour to it. "*Real* bad news, I'm afraid."

He spent the night *again* last night, and it should feel like too much too soon, but somehow it doesn't.

He was a welcome sight in my home, and he slotted in with such ease. I don't think Ethan or I felt like we had a guest – he just felt like part of our day to day life.

"I just got off the phone with Officer Cleland; he checked out the car registered to Mr. Johnathan Orlando and—"

"That's his name, Johnathan Orlando?" I interrupt him.

"Yeah, Morgs, that's him."

"That sounds like such a normal name."

"I wish," he mutters, "anyway, they checked out his vehicles. He's got two cars, a bright-red convertible and a white sports car."

My stomach sinks.

I instinctively check my rear-view mirror, but this is a busy street, and I can't look at every car that passes by. There's a white car a few cars behind me, but it's an SUV.

I breathe out, then back in sharply when I glance in front of me again.

There's a red car on the other side of the intersection, but it's not a convertible.

"What are we meant to do?" I ask quietly.

"He offered to send a patrol car past his place a couple of times a day – it won't achieve a lot, but it might make their presence felt – make him think twice before he gets any ideas."

"That's a good idea," I reply, somewhat numbly as I turn off the main highway.

My eyes flick to my mirror, but there's only black and silver behind me.

"It'll be okay, Morgs, I promise you," he says softly, and it melts me.

I'm not sure I believe it will be okay, but when he says it, I believe him.

"You're having Jerome meet you at the house, right?" he asks, and I nod, even though he can't see me.

"Yeah, he'll be there."

"Okay, good, I have to go into the gym this morning, but I can be anywhere you need me after that, okay?"

I nod again. "I just need you with me."

"I like the sound of that," he replies, and I can tell he's smiling. "I'm meant to be going to Liv's for dinner tonight, do you and Ethan want to come?"

"I'd actually love that," I reply, relieved as I turn onto the quiet street that houses the home I'm trying to sell.

I'm the only car that turns this way, and I'm glad.

As much as I don't want to be alone, I also don't want to look in that mirror another time and feel fear.

"It's a date then. I'll swing by your place around half five and we can head off when you're ready…"

I know he's still talking, but I can't hear anything other than the whooshing of my heartbeat in my ears as I pull up outside the house.

"Oh my god," I breathe.

"What?"

I cover my mouth, the only sound escaping is a horrified gasp.

"Morgan, what is it?" he demands.

I can't believe what I'm seeing.

"Someone has spray-painted my sign," I whisper as I stare, *horrified*, at the huge sign advertising the house for sale, complete with a picture of my face, now with the added detail of the word 'cock tease' plastered across it.

I tell Brody what I'm seeing, and a deep, feral snarl comes through my car's Bluetooth.

"Don't touch it," he demands. "Is your assistant there yet?"

The sound of an engine behind me startles me, but when I look back, I see the familiar car – a green station wagon that Jerome drives.

"He just got here."

"Good. Get him to sit in the car with you – do not go in the house – I'm calling the police."

"Alright," I whisper, "I'll wait."

"I have to hang up, baby, to make the call," he replies softly.

"Right." I nod, dazed. "Of course."

"Are the homeowners around?"

I shake my head. "They went on holiday for two weeks."

"Alright, I'll call you back, baby, okay?"

"Alright." I swallow deeply.

"It'll be okay," he promises.

I don't reply.

"Oh and, Morgs?" he questions before I can hang up.

"Yeah?"

"I love you."

I gasp, I think that might have shocked me more than the graffiti I just saw.

I don't get time to reply before the line goes dead.

***

"So, what are you going to do about this?" Brody demands of the officer who was sent out to handle the situation. "No one can call this a coincidence now, can they?"

I shift my weight from foot to foot.

The past two hours have passed in a blur. This poor officer, whose name I can't even remember, turned up about twenty minutes after I got off the phone with Brody.

He dusted for prints, instructed Jerome to take the sign down and then checked the house for any sign of intrusion.

He found none, so I was given the go ahead to host my open home, all the while, my heart was beating so fast, the people viewing probably thought I was on speed.

Brody turned up ten minutes ago, full of rage and pent-up energy.

The officer – who was told to sit in his car out on the street until I was finished – has been doing his best to placate him, but it's not really working. Brody wants answers, and he wants them now.

He also loves me, so there's that.

I reach out and take his hand in mine. His fingers grip tight, but he doesn't look at me.

"I assure you, sir, we're taking this very seriously."

"As you should be, my girlfriend is being *stalked*."

I feel bad for this poor officer; he's had to deal with me – borderline hysterical – and now he's having to mollify my overly protective boyfriend.

"Have you talked to the neighbours?" Brody demands.

He tugs on my arm, dragging me closer and nestling me against him – apparently deciding that I wasn't quite close enough.

"I've spoken to everyone that was home, and there is one report of interest, a car parked outside the house sometime in the early hours of the morning, a man exited the car for a period of time, before getting back in and driving away – the resident mentioned the excessive speed."

"Well that's got to be him. Let me guess, a white car?"

The officer nods. "It was dark out so the witness couldn't be sure, but the car was light in colour, so white, silver or grey probably and the man was described as being tall and broad, wearing dark clothing and something on his head – she thought maybe a cap."

"I assume she didn't get a plate?" I ask.

The officer shakes his head. "Unfortunately, it was too dark and happened too quickly."

I sigh. I just feel drained.

I just want this whole thing to be over.

"Do you think I should get a restraining order?"

"I think that would be wise at this point," the officer tells me at the same time Brody replies, "Fuck yes you should. Why haven't we done that already?"

"Because words on a piece of paper don't stop crazy people? Because nothing has actually happened to me? Because a couple of prank calls and white cars being on the road isn't actually the same as being threatened?" I insist.

Brody scowls at me. "Some dude just tagged a sign with your face on it; I think we've entered new territory."

"I agree, and I doubt a restraining order will help, but I'll get it anyway."

Brody looks at the officer pointedly. "Well you heard her, she said she'll get it anyway."

I nudge him in the side. "It's not his fault," I hiss.

He smirks, actually smirks down at me with that sexy smile of his. "Never said it was, baby, and as long as he does his job, we won't have any problems."

I shoot the officer an apologetic glance.

"I've got all of your details, Ms. Bradley, I'll be in touch when we have something for you to sign."

"Thank you," I reply.

Brody just scowls as he watches him leave.

"I should call Ethan," I mutter.

"He's fine. He was at the gym when I left, running drills with Adam."

"He's at the gym?" I question, my brain feeling fuzzy, I'm sure that he didn't have training today. "What's he doing at the gym?"

"I asked him to come down after school, so I knew where he was."

Tingles race up and down my spine.

He didn't just think of me, he thought of my son too.

"You were worried about him?"

He frowns at me. "Of course, I was, there's a crazy dude on the loose and –"

I interrupt him by crashing my mouth to his, kissing him with everything I have – relief, gratitude, fear, trust...

"What was that for?" He chuckles as we break apart and he swipes a stray blonde curl from my face.

I shrug. "It was just because I love you too."

CHAPTER EIGHTEEN

Brody

"Relax, baby, he's fine... Chad's an asshole, but he's probably taken him to the most expensive restaurant in town to show off what a 'good guy' he is. He's fine, trust me."

She huffs out a laugh and puts her phone down. "He'll be in for a shock when the bill comes if that's the case – that kid eats like a horse."

I chuckle. I hope he does. Paying a ridiculously expensive bill is the least Chad could do after all these years of not being a father.

"Come outside with me." I get to my feet and hold my hand out for her to take.

"I should help Liv clean up," she argues, her eyes drifting to where Liv and Adam are in the kitchen cleaning up and arguing.

"Nah, Adam lost a bet, clean-up is all his."

Morgan grins at the idea of that, she might not know him well, but she knows enough to know that he's the competitive type who doesn't lose well. "What'd he lose?"

"Liv bet him he couldn't make two shots in a row from the midcourt line. He thought he could. He was wrong." I laugh.

She takes my hand and lets me lead her towards the door off the back of the living area. "So, why's she in there helping if he lost?"

"Because," I tap the end of her nose, "my sister is a control freak."

"I heard that," Liv yells from the kitchen.

"And she has supersonic hearing too apparently," I grumble as Morgan giggles.

I slide the door open and usher her out, snagging a blanket off the chair by the door as we go out.

"You kids be safe out there," Adam yells after us as he throws his arm around Liv's shoulders. "They grow up so fast," he says to her.

She rolls her eyes and shrugs off his arm.

I chuckle. Adam never tires of winding up my sister.

"C'mon." I tug Morgan's hand and she follows me onto the deck, down the stairs until we're on the lawn. I lie the blanket down and gesture for her to sit.

She smiles sweetly at me, her beautiful green eyes sparkling in the moonlight.

"It's pretty out here," she breathes as I lie down on the blanket next to her.

I tug her arm and she lies down too, snuggling into my side.

I point up in the sky at the stars and she whispers, "Wow."

"You can see them better from here than at my place."

"Must be all those big fancy houses in your way," she teases.

She points to the sky and traces shapes with her fingers. "It's like doing one of those join the dot pictures you used to do as a kid."

I chuckle and kiss her forehead.

She keeps moving her finger through the air, me watching, trying to guess what she's drawing for a while longer before her hand drops back down onto my chest.

"Thank you for today," she says softly.

My breath catches for a moment before evening out again. "I didn't do anything."

"You did. You took me to the station to sort out the restraining order, you made sure that Ethan was somewhere safe... you called the cops in the first place."

"All within the realms of being a decent boyfriend."

"You held my hand... made sure I knew everything was okay," she whispers.

"You're always safe with me, you don't need to thank me for it."

"Can't you just stop arguing and say you're welcome?"

I chuckle. "Alright. You're welcome."

She smiles, seemingly satisfied. "Finally, now are you going to let me thank you properly, or what?"

I don't know if she's suggesting anything that should get my dirty mind racing or not, but that doesn't stop it from going there anyway.

"What did you have in mind?" I choke out through images of her in wicked positions.

She leans up and whispers in my ear, and *fuck*, if I thought my mind was dirty, then hers is filthy.

My jaw drops open and she giggles.

"What do you think?" She batts her long lashes at me innocently.

"I think that I don't know what the fuck we're still doing at my sister's house."

She bites into her bottom lip and trails her hand ever so slowly down my chest. She runs her fingers over my stomach and lower to the fly of my jeans.

"Who said we have to leave to have fun?"

I swallow deeply.

My hips lift on their own accord as she undoes the button and slides the zipper down.

I'm in my sister's back yard – I should definitely not be thinking about all the different ways I could fuck my girlfriend right now, but I am. I guess even grown men are horny teenage boys on the inside.

"*Morgs*," I groan as she slips her small, warm hand into first my jeans, and then inside my boxer briefs.

I glance up at the deck we've just come down from, but there's no sign of Adam or Liv. If I'd known we were going to get hot and heavy down here I would have grabbed a second blanket.

She grips tighter and a deep hum comes from deep in my throat, my head falls back against the blanket as she strokes my growing erection from base to tip.

"I think we should go back to your place," I groan as I feel myself growing.

She giggles, her lips pressing to my neck over and over again.

My hips thrust again, in time with each slow, languid stroke.

My hand finds her hip and drags downwards towards the bottom of her dress, my fingers skimming back up her thigh until I reach the fabric of her underwear.

She gasps in surprise but spreads her legs a little wider to allow me to tug her underwear to the side and rub my thumb over her most sensitive spots.

"I'm meant to be the one thanking you," she murmurs.

"Trust me, baby, this *is* you thanking me," I growl as I slip two fingers inside her.

Her back arches off the blanket and her eyes flutter closed as I work her slowly, my thumb circling her clit.

She moans, and I don't give a fuck where I am anymore. I roll off her, her hand falling from my dick, and tug my jeans down enough so I can slip it out of my pants.

I hover over her, still torturing her with my fingers, and she looks up at me with wide eyes.

I slowly pull out of her. "Roll over," I say.

She does as I say, scrambling to her knees and turning so her ass is facing me.

I grab her ankles and drag her backwards, so her feet are on either side of my knees, her ass high in the air.

"Did you think I wouldn't screw you on my sister's lawn?" I growl.

She twists back to look at me over her shoulder, a devious smile on her face. "Actually, I was *really* hoping you would."

I chuckle. "What's going to happen if someone walks out?"

I hook my finger into her underwear and shift them to the side. I line up and slam into her hard.

She moans. Loudly. Really fucking loudly.

I pull out nearly to the tip before pushing back in again. "Huh, Morgs?" I say through clenched teeth. "You like the idea of getting caught?"

"I don't dislike it," she says through shaky breaths.

Fuck, I don't dislike it either, I'm ready to blow.

I keep up my relentless pace, until she says my name like a plea, and that's when I know she's there.

I slam into her once more and we both fall off the edge together.

CHAPTER NINETEEN

Morgan

"How did it go with your dad last night?" I ask as I sip my morning coffee.

I didn't get to see Ethan when we got home last night.

We spent half the night at Olivia's, and then took a moonlit walk along the beach before going home.

I feel my cheeks blush as I think about letting Brody fuck me in his sister's back yard.

I blush even harder when I think about how I got on my knees and really thanked him at the beach later on.

I clear my throat and turn to busy myself in the sink so that Ethan won't see the redness on my cheeks.

"It was alright," he replies between mouthfuls of cereal.

"Where did he take you?"

"That new place downtown, you know the one with the huge sign out front that you said would cost a bomb?"

I grin to myself. Brody was right.

"Was the food good?" I ask.

It's hard not to ask, 'did your dad act like a prick?', because that's what I imagine the evening was like.

"Yeah," he replies.

I turn back to face him, leaning my hip against the bench.

"Is everything alright?"

He glances up at me before looking back at his food. "Yeah, it's just Dad... you know? I don't think he really listens to anything I say. He asks questions, but somehow we always end up talking about football."

My heart breaks a little bit hearing that.

I know exactly what Ethan means, and he's right. Chad's number one priority has always been football.

"I don't even like football." He sighs.

"You know what, bud? Neither do I." I step forward and ruffle his hair, and he pulls away, a grin on his face.

"Mum! You're wrecking my hair."

Just about anything would be an improvement on that comb-over style he's still sporting, but I don't pester him with it today.

I hear a yawn behind me and spin around to see what is quite possibly the sexiest sight I've ever seen.

Brody is wearing grey sweatpants, slung low on his hips, and no shirt.

"Dude! We had a deal," Ethan groans.

Brody chuckles and runs a hand through his hair. "Sorry, bro."

He reaches behind himself, tugs a t-shirt out from the back of his waistband and shrugs it on.

I pout.

He chuckles as he passes me, snagging the cup of coffee out of my hand as he goes.

I scowl at him, but my irritation is short-lived.

"Wanna go shoot some hoops?" Brody asks. "Work on your three-point shots?"

Ethan's head snaps up and he grins. "Really?"

"Yeah?" Brody frowns at him as though he doesn't see what the big deal is, but I see it.

Ethan has just spent an entire evening with the man who fathered him, and I doubt he showed him even one second of genuine attention.

"Cool." Ethan grins.

Brody shakes his head in amusement.

"Meet you out front," Ethan announces as he races away from his bowl, and down the hallway to find his shoes.

I can't hide the huge smile on my face, so I turn away and make myself a replacement coffee.

I feel, rather than hear him come up behind me, before his long, lean arms wrap around me from behind, his chin coming to rest on my shoulder.

"Good coffee, baby," he says, his voice husky.

I smack at his hand as he reaches for the sugar.

He chuckles. "It alright with you if we go shoot some hoops?"

"It's more than alright," I say, my voice cracking.

"Morgs?" he questions.

I shake my head. "I'm good." I take a deep breath and try to reign in the crazy mumma bear shit. "I'm just really thankful that you're here, Coach Owens," I say with a grin.

"That makes two of us," he says before he kisses my cheek and lets me go.

I pour myself a coffee and head out to watch my two favourite boys play some ball.

***

Ethan is practically bouncing in the backseat.

It's their first real game of the season tonight, and the kid is pumped.

Brody had to tell him to stop practising; he spent the better part of the day out front bouncing that damn ball against the concrete.

At least it gave Brody and me some time alone inside.

He hasn't let me out of his sight for longer than five minutes since he arrived at the open home to see the graffiti for himself.

There's protective, and then there's Brody, but honestly, I wouldn't have it any other way.

I love having him around.

I spent a long time carefully constructing walls around my heart, and Brody broke them all down within a matter of days.

I think he could move in with me and I wouldn't even bat an eyelid about it.

Ethan might grumble about our PDAs, but I think he likes having a decent man around as much as I do.

We pull up to the gym; the car park has a few stray cars here and there, but given that we're here this early, I didn't expect to find it full.

It's not until I shut off the engine that I realise I didn't check for cars following me, not once – not with Brody in the car next to me.

"I'm going to see if Hunter is here yet," Ethan calls out.

I don't even know if the car was stopped before he opened his door and climbed out, but he's gone, his basketball under his arm as he jogs towards the entrance.

If I didn't know better, I'd think that thing was glued to him.

"So, he's excited." Brody chuckles.

"What makes you think that?" I grin as I climb out of the car.

He grabs a huge bag that he pulled from the boot of his car before we left home, swings it over his shoulder, his other arm coming around me and tugging me against his side.

I love the way he can make my heart race, just by doing something so simple.

"You've got a bit of a wait until the game, Morgs," Brody says as he opens the door to the gym for me.

I slide my phone out of my pocket and wave it at him. "Lucky I stocked up my kindle before we left the house."

Hunter is nowhere to be seen, but Ethan is inside the gym already, bouncing his ball around the court with a man that I quickly recognise as Adam.

"Is he here for the game?" I question.

Brody nods and grins. "I had to agree to buy him dinner next weekend to get him to come, but honestly, I think he played me – he's got a bit of a soft spot for the kids."

"They're going to freak."

"I think a few of my other old teammates were going to get down too, so it should be a good motivator for the boys."

"I know what you're doing." I point a finger at him. "You're trying to get me to thank you again."

He chuckles. "A guy can dream."

***

My throat is starting to hurt from cheering so loudly.

We're into the fourth and final quarter, and Ethan's team is up by five points. It's a tight game – Brody hasn't stopped pacing the side of court, yelling out plays and tips to the boys.

Ethan makes a steal and tears off down the court with the ball, his teammates on the bench screaming at him.

He's got all the space in the world to make an easy two points here, but instead he looks back, finds Hunter and fires the ball at him.

He bounces it twice, lines up the shot and the ball swishes through the basket for three points.

The two boys high five one another as they run back down the court.

That's one thing I learned pretty quickly about basketball – they high five every fifteen seconds. Every play, basket, free throw... anything – they're there high fiving, there's even the occasional butt tap.

Ethan is subbed out and my heart warms as I watch Brody praising him, clapping him on the shoulder as he collapses into a chair to watch.

"Yeah, Ethan!" I yell, because today I'm one of those sports mums that can't keep their mouths shut.

Chad turns around from his spot in front of me, two rows down and raises his brows at me, his lip twitching in amusement.

I barely resist the urge to show him my middle finger.

At least he's here I guess, it's more than I expected. In fact, now that I think about it, this is the first game he's ever been to.

Maybe he is planning to make more of an effort.

Maybe he's just trying to piss me off.

I'm not sure I care either way.

I don't know how long he's planning to stay in town for, but I'm over it.

He had another go at Brody before the game about staying away from 'his woman', and he's been doing his best to flirt with me any chance he gets. I had to move up and put an extra row between us just to get some space.

Isabella nudges my knee. "I can't believe *that* is your ex."

I clench my jaw. "Trust me, there's a good reason he's the ex and not the current."

She sighs wistfully. "There *always* is, and points for staying strong. I'm not sure how strong I'd be if a man looking like that came knocking on my door." She fans her face dramatically.

"He's all yours," I mumble as I try to distract myself with the game.

Brody is still stalking up and down the side of the court, pointing every so often and throwing his arms up in outrage if the ref's call doesn't go his team's way.

Basketball coaches sure are passionate.

I feel my phone vibrate in the pocket of my jacket and I slide it out, only half paying attention.

I click on the message, cheering as the Tigers make another shot.

I glance down at my phone and my blood runs cold.

It's those same two words.

'Cock tease'.

That's all it says.

I don't recognise the number.

"Oh my god," I breathe.

I've barely uttered the words when another message comes through, and this time a whimper escapes my lips.

'I like you in green. Brings out your eyes.'

I glance down at the green jacket I'm wearing.

He's *here*.

"Are you alright?" Isabella asks.

I shake my head as I show her the screen of my phone. "I'm being stalked."

She gasps, her hand coming up to cover her mouth as she reads the words. "I'll get Brody."

"No," I reply quickly, my hand coming down on her arm. "The game isn't over."

I glance up at the clock. There's only two minutes left.

My eyes scan the crowd, looking for the guy from the bar, but it's no use, there are people everywhere, the stands are packed. There's as many people behind me as there are in front of me – I'd never spot him – I barely even remember what he looked like.

"Morgan!" Isabella yells, and I shake my head to clear my thoughts. I don't know how many times she said my name.

I look at her with wide eyes.

"Are you okay, do you think we should leave? Or call the police or something?"

"No." I shake my head. "We should wait for Brody." I don't know what to do, but I do know that I won't do anything or go anywhere without him.

I can feel the colour draining from my face as I think about what could happen here.

I could be in real danger.

He's close enough to know what I'm wearing.

A shiver passes over my skin as I look around the crowd.

Chad turns around again and my eyes meet his.

He frowns and turns to rest in the empty space on the row between us as he takes in the expression on my face.

"Are you okay, princess?"

"Don't call me princess," I reply automatically.

"Morgan, what's going on?"

I really must look terrified if he's willing to not annoy me to get an answer.

"She's being stalked," Isabella blurts out, and I could slap her.

The last thing I need is Chad in my business.

"What?" he replies, outraged, his eyes shifting from her to me, "you're being stalked?"

"Maybe. I'm not sure," I reply, my voice barely more than a whisper as my gaze travels from the face of the man I used to love down to the court in search of the man I love now.

The final buzzer sounds, and I get to my feet.

I hear Isabella and Chad both speaking, but I don't hear what they're saying; I don't really care, I just want Brody.

I want his protection. I want him to wrap his arms around me like a safety net and keep me out of harm's way.

I jog down the steps, muttering 'excuse me' and 'sorry' to everyone I shove past.

I finally make it onto the courtside and I slip past the crowds of people that are making their way out of the gym.

I push up to my tip toes and catch sight of his thick head of dark hair on the court.

I almost cry in relief. I'm nearly there.

The crowd opens up, and I stumble through the gap and onto the court.

Brody is just giving the last boy in the line a high five, a huge grin on his face, when his gaze lands on me.

His grin drops as he takes me in.

I blow out a deep breath, I didn't realise I'd been holding it in.

He strides toward me, his long legs carrying him quickly, closing the gap between us in seconds.

"Morgs," he mutters as he wraps his arms around me tightly, tugging me against him.

"Something happened," I choke out. "I'm scared."

He doesn't speak for a few beats, just holds me tight as people file out of the gym in throngs.

"Adam!" Brody finally yells out.

I hear someone approach, but I don't lift my face from the front of Brody's shirt.

"What's going on?"

"Give Anthony a hand to take the boys for a warm down, will you?" Brody asks, his deep voice vibrating in his chest.

"Everything alright?"

I feel Brody moving, shaking his head I assume. "I don't think so."

I hear Adam jog away and call out to the team and then I'm moving, being walked on numb legs, tucked against my pillar of strength.

I hear him open a door, then close it behind us.

He presses my shoulders down until I'm sitting.

He pries me from his chest, his finger hooking under my chin so that I have to look at him.

"Tell me what happened," he demands.

CHAPTER TWENTY

Brody

I run my hand through my hair and check again that I can still see her sitting in the office with Hunter's mum.

I know she's still there – she couldn't go anywhere if she tried, I locked her in, but still... it hasn't stopped me from checking every fifteen seconds.

That fucker is going to pay for scaring her like this.

I'm going to make him pay.

Anthony, my assistant coach, and Adam are still putting the boys through the warm down. They're all buzzing with excitement over their first win – I was too, until I saw her face.

Ethan jogs over to me, frowning in confusion at his mum in the office.

"What's wrong with Mum?" he demands.

I don't know how much Morgan has told him, but he's sixteen, I think he's old enough to know at least some of the truth. It's probably not my decision to make, but I'm making it anyway. Ethan might be a teenager, but he's tall and strong – he could protect Morgan if it came to it, I need to be able to count on him.

"Someone is scaring your mum, sending her text messages and stuff."

He frowns. "Is it whoever wrote that shit on one of her signs?"

I raise a brow at him. I know Morgan didn't tell him about that.

"I heard her on the phone," he explains, "and then Jerome put the sign in our garage, spray paint on it and all…"

I nod. I guess he knows more than I thought.

"It's the same person," I tell him.

"Is she okay?" he asks, his eyes flickering with concern as he glances back towards the office.

"She'll be alright, bud," I promise him as I clap him on the shoulder. "She's got me and you to watch her back, right?"

He shoots me a small smile. "Right."

"I won't let anything happen to her, Ethan, I'm not going to run away when things get tough. It's not who I am."

He nods gratefully.

"Go finish up with the guys."

He turns, his gaze lingering on the stand, before running back to join his teammates.

I follow where he looked, and find that Chad is still here, and he's chatting up the mums by the looks.

I don't know why he's stayed behind, but just the fact that he's here makes me want to punch something – preferably him.

He must feel my eyes on him because he turns, then gets to his feet and heads in my direction.

"Fuck's sake," I mutter.

This is not what I need right now.

I cross the court to meet him, so we're further away from my team when we come face to face.

He smirks arrogantly at me as he approaches.

"Chad." I nod.

"*Coach*," he retorts. It fucks me off that he refuses to address me by name, but I don't show my irritation – that's what he wants.

"Not bad," he says, and the urge to punch him grows stronger.

"What do you want?" I cross my arms across my chest.

He has something to say, that much is obvious, so we may as well get on with it.

"Nothing." He shrugs, but I'm not buying it. "In fact, I was just about to leave – I'll just check on Morgan and I'll be on my way."

He steps towards the office, and I step with him, blocking his path, my arms falling to my sides. "Like hell you will."

His brows rise a fraction. "Excuse me?"

"I said, *like hell*. You're not going anywhere near her."

"She's the mother of my child, and if I want to see her, I will," he says, his jaw tight.

I shake my head. "That ship has sailed, Jenson, she's not at your beck and call anymore. She's moved on and you need to do what you do best and just disappear."

He laughs, as though I said something hilariously funny, and my fists ball up tight.

He takes another step, towards me this time and sneers at me. "You really think I'm going to let some washed-up basketball player tell *me* what to do? I'm Chad fucking Jenson, and I answer to no one."

I step forward too, so our chests almost touch.

"You try me, see what happens," I offer.

His eyes harden and I'm about half a second away from cracking when I feel a heavy hand rest on my shoulder.

Chad's eyes move from mine to the man over my shoulder who I already know is Adam.

"Got a problem here, man?" Adam asks, and somehow it manages to sound like a threat.

Chad Jenson might be a prick, but he's no idiot. He knows we've got him beat.

He steps back, huffs out a laugh, and turns around to leave without saying a word.

I'm fucking furious about what just happened, but not as mad as I am that he left without even congratulating Ethan on the incredible game he just played.

I consider going after him, but Adam's hand on my shoulder stops me.

"Not here," he warns.

He's right. This isn't the time or the place.

I have to set an example for the boys, and fighting isn't what I'm here to teach them.

"You all good?" Adam asks.

I nod my head, my anger fizzling out somewhat. "I'm good."

"Let's get this wrapped up so you can take care of your girl."

"Yeah," I reply. That's the only thing I can think about doing.

***

"Cheers, Adam, I appreciate the help," I say as we walk out of the gym, Morgan fused to my side and Ethan doing what he always does, bouncing his ball and flipping that fucking ridiculous blonde hair from his face.

I don't know how he plays like that, but he seems to have it sorted.

"Don't sweat it, just get your wallet ready for that dinner you owe me, bro." He rubs his hands together eagerly.

The guy makes a high six-figure salary these days, but he's never stopped trying to get free shit.

I wave out to him as he crosses the carpark in the opposite direction.

"Later, Adam!" Ethan yells after him.

Adam throws him a hang loose.

"You okay?" I ask Morgan quietly, so that Ethan can't hear.

She looks up at me, her green eyes still wide with fear. "I just feel so... *violated.*"

I know what she means, I feel the same way.

I also feel angry, really fucking angry.

Ethan jogs off ahead, still practising his moves. I swear the kid never stops.

"We'll swing by your place to get you guys some stuff, then I'm taking you back to my house."

She doesn't argue, just nods her head and snuggles in even closer to me.

"Hey." I reach down and tip her chin so she has to look at me. "I love you."

"I love you too," she says, the corners of her mouth finally lifting.

I take the opportunity to kiss her.

"Um, Mum..." Ethan's voice breaks the moment.

I glance up and my stomach drops. Scrawled across the front of her windscreen, written in god only knows what, are the words 'cock tease'.

I hear Morgan gasp and then a sob rips from her throat.

"Ethan, come stay with your mum," I tell him calmly, even though I feel anything but.

He nods his head, his own eyes now wide and shaken.

I pry Morgan from my side and Ethan holds his arms out to hug her.

He really is a good kid.

I shrug the bag off my shoulder and pull out a few of the left-over water bottles and some of the sweat towels that I need to drop to the dry cleaners.

I pour the water on the windscreen and scrub at the bull-shit words with the towels, anger radiating from me.

Cock tease. She's nothing of the fucking sort.

I could kill him.

I could literally kill him for this.

I rub at the windscreen with all the aggression inside me, and when I'm done, I'm much calmer; I'm the man Morgan needs.

I toss the gear in the boot, scoop Morgan into my arms and carry her to the passenger seat.

I buckle her up and kiss her forehead. "I'll fix this, baby, I promise."

CHAPTER TWENTY-ONE

Morgan

"I don't like it, Morgs."

I don't particularly like it either, but unfortunately, it's my job. I can't just turn down clients because I'm shaken and scared.

I'm all cried out now at least, so I'm less likely to break down in public.

I spent half the night bawling.

Brody got us home, ordered in some takeout, which kept Ethan happy, and then the two of them proceeded to look at me with concern and treat me with kid gloves until I couldn't handle it anymore and went to bed.

He wanted us to go to his place for the night, but I think he could see I was too exhausted to make that happen, so he stayed with us instead.

Brody held me in his arms as I sobbed and promised me over and over again that he'd take care of me – that nothing was going to happen to me on his watch.

I believe him. I know he'd never stand back and let anyone hurt me, but he isn't there with me all the time, and that's when I feel most vulnerable.

I watch Brody pace the room again and catch his arm to stop him as he passes me.

"I'll be *fine*. It's just a house viewing."

Nothing bad can happen there, the place isn't even on the market yet – no one could possibly have set anything up there. There's no sign with my name on it, no paper trail, *nothing*.

"Who are you meeting there?" he asks with his brows furrowed.

"A nice family that I showed through a house last week. They didn't want to make an offer and I think this place will be a better fit for them."

"So, you've met them before?"

"Yes." I sigh.

"And is Jerome meeting you there?"

I shake my head. "He's picking me up from here. I thought that seemed like a better idea."

He nods in approval. "Alright."

"Yeah?" I ask cautiously. I don't want to believe that I've won the battle prematurely.

He's been adamant all morning that he was coming with me to work – which normally wouldn't be the worst thing in the world, but with his current on-edge state, I couldn't have him sniffing around. He'd scare off my buyer.

"I would have preferred that we heard back from Officer Cleland before you left, but apparently those cops are on their own clock," he grumbles.

I refrain from laughing. It's not even nine yet. He called late last night, putting whoever the poor sucker answering the phones was on blast, ranting and raving and demanding that they do something.

We're waiting to hear back.

"He's not going to be able to tell us anything." I try to soothe him, but it's no use, he's back pacing the room.

"Surely they can arrest him for this."

I'd love for that to happen, but unfortunately, we have no proof that he did anything at all to me, and when it comes down to it, I haven't actually been threatened.

The number the texts came from must have been a throwaway because when Brody tried to call it back, the line was dead.

Even the police aren't going to be able to do anything with that.

"I guess we'll find out when we hear back," I reply and I can hear my voice shake.

He stops pacing, strides across the room and envelopes me in his embrace, crushing his lips to mine in a kiss so passionate it takes my breath away.

He's got me in his arms, edging my ass onto the countertop before I can even say his name.

"I'm sorry," he says against my lips before shifting his focus to my neck and throat.

"Sorry for what?" I tilt my head to allow him better access, my voice a breathy moan.

"For being so crazy. I just can't stand the thought of anything happening to you, Morgs. I really do love you."

He brings his face back to mine, his unkempt facial hair gently scratching my chin.

He rests his forehead against mine. "I know I haven't told you that properly yet, but I love you, so damn much."

"I love you too," I whisper, my heart thumping in my chest. "You make me feel like the most important person in the world."

"You are." He rubs his nose against mine. "If you could see yourself through my eyes, you wouldn't doubt it, not for a second."

***

"Lover boy was a bit on edge this morning," Jerome says, his brow raised at me as he navigates the streets to the house we're scheduled to show.

"Mmm hmm," I agree, unwilling to say anything more.

He was well on edge, but not without good reason I remind myself.

He laughs. "So... has he moved in with you now or what?"

I shake my head, but honestly, it feels a little bit like we're living together. He won't hear of me spending the night alone.

"I'm not sure," I admit, "honestly, I think if we were moving in, it'd be to his house not mine. That place is *nice*." I grin.

"You should go for it. He's seems cool – you know, when he's not acting crazy."

Jerome had a front-row seat to Brody's performance at the house the other day when we found the graffiti and got the police involved. He knows *exactly* how protective my boyfriend is.

I just shake my head in amusement.

"He can chill, I've got your back today."

"I'm very reassured," I mutter under my breath.

Jerome isn't exactly built the way Brody is. I'm not sure if physically he'd be any more use than me if it came down to it, but I'm grateful for his company nonetheless.

I really do feel good about today though.

He pulls up at the house and we're greeted with nothing but a peaceful neighbourhood.

There's no graffiti, no calls, no texts, *nothing* for the entire viewing, and when it's time to leave, we've even got an offer to present to our client – I was right, everything was fine here.

"Well, you can call him and let him know that everything went just great." Jerome chuckles as he buckles his seatbelt so we can head back home.

I roll my eyes at him, but I *do* want to call Brody. He promised not to call me before I contacted him – I didn't need him checking on me halfway through the viewing.

I hit call on his number and wait.

The phone rings only twice before he answers, "*Morgs*, thank god."

I huff out a laugh. "Hello to you too."

"Hey, baby, sorry, but look – we have another problem."

I take a deep breath. I'm so god damn over this. It's just one thing after another.

A call starts coming in on my cell, but I hit ignore, whoever that is can wait.

"What's going on now?"

I glance at Jerome warily and he shoots me a sympathetic look. Seconds later, his phone starts ringing and he pulls over to answer it.

"It's the guy from the bar."

"Are you okay? Is Ethan—"

"I'm fine. Ethan is at school. I'll call him after his next class. He'll be fine," he interrupts me. "But, Morgs, Jonathon Orlando *wasn't* the one who text you last night, or wrote that shit on your car... the police got what they needed to take him into custody yesterday. He's been in a holding cell with no cell phone for the past twenty-four hours."

"*What?*" I gape. "But the words, they're the same as the sign..."

"Which means it was probably never him," he says quietly. He sounds defeated.

"I don't know what to say."

Jerome tugs on my sleeve and looks at me like he has something he needs to say.

"Give me one sec, slick, okay?"

I hold my phone away from my mouth.

"What's up?" I ask. I notice we're no longer heading in the direction of my house.

"That was Russell, he tried to call you first, he's had a family emergency and asked if we could take over his open home, it's over the other side of town – multimillion-dollar property." He glances at his watch. "It's like, right now."

I groan, but I already know I'll say yes. "Fine, fine, let's just try make it quick. Hopefully all the rich people are busy today."

He nods and moves the car a little faster.

"Brody?" I question.

"I don't like it, Morgs," he says, the same as he did before I left this morning. He obviously heard our conversation.

"It'll be fine. An expensive property like that, one with alarms and security cameras is the least of my worries. In fact, if I could hang out there all day, it would probably be the best place for me."

"You'll hang out nowhere but with me," he growls. "I've got plenty of ways to keep you busy."

"Alright, slick," I reply, my teeth sinking into my lip. "I like the sound of that."

"Be careful," he says as we round the corner and drive down one of the most expensive streets in town.

***

"I can't believe they literally left the key under the door mat; rich people sure don't give a fuck, do they?"

I laugh, but don't bother reminding him that we had to get through a pin-coded gate and past a bunch of security cameras just to get near the front door.

"I think I hear a car," he says, leaning towards the front door.

"Alright, you go welcome them, I'll just get this information set up and we'll be good to go."

He nods and heads off out the front door, straightening his jacket as he goes.

I glance out the window as I hear the rumble of an engine, and what I see makes me shiver.

It's a white sports car. Just like the one I was convinced was following me.

It pulls up to a stop, the silver horse on the front shining in the sunlight, and I gasp.

"Jerome," I say, but my voice is barely above a whisper.

I watch on in horror as a man steps out of the car.

That horror turns to disbelief as I realise, I know this man. It's Chad.

It all clicks in my head. It's Chad. It's been Chad the whole time. This shit started when he turned up.

I consider running. He might have been stalking me, but I doubt he knows I'm here right now – he couldn't possibly, this was completely last minute, and filling in for a work colleague is something I hardly ever have to do.

Unless he's tracking me, this isn't part of his plan.

I clutch my chest and consider ringing Brody, but I can't. I can hear voices now, and they're coming closer.

"Come on in, leave your shoes on, the polished concrete floors are very forgiving, Morgan is just inside."

"*Morgan*?" I hear Chad ask, and my heart thumps so loud I can feel it in my ears.

I don't know what he's doing here – why he's looking at a house in *my* town, the town I fled to, to escape *him*.

"Yes, sorry, Russell has had an emergency, he's asked Morgan to fill in."

Jerome steps into view, Chad's blonde head visible now behind him.

I'm shaking.

I don't know what the hell to do.

He's been stalking me, calling me a cock tease, all the while flirting with me to my face, hurting my son and threatening my boyfriend.

I suck in a deep breath as Chad steps into the room and his gaze falls on me.

He looks shocked, and I hope he is, because the game is over now.

He's stooped low over the years, but this is a new one.

I'm about to open my mouth and scream at him when another blonde head catches my attention.

Chad *isn't* alone. Clasping his arm in hers is a petite blonde woman, with a very pregnant-looking belly and a huge shiny ring on her finger.

"Morgan, this is Chad and Penny," Jerome introduces me.

The woman on my ex's arm stares at me, but I can't say anything. I look back to Chad, to see what he'll do, but he just stares back at me, waiting for my reaction.

Penny giggles. "I'm so sorry, sweetie, we should have sent a warning or something, I guess it's not every day you get a superstar like my husband walk into your open homes."

"Husband?" I question, and I don't know why I even care, but that's the word that falls from my mouth.

"Been married four years," she replies proudly.

"Morgan, right? It's nice to meet you." Chad steps forward, his hand extended. He looks nervous. I don't know what to make of it.

I gape at him, and without conscious thought I find myself shaking his hand, rather than clawing his eyes out.

He's pretending. For *her.*

His *wife* doesn't know who I am.

I wonder if she even knows he has another child.

I wonder if she even knows why they're here.

"I... um... I... I need to make a phone call," I stutter.

"Let me show you around," Jerome suggests, gesturing for the two of them to follow him. He shoots me a look over his shoulder, but I can't respond.

Chad turns away from me, and I honestly don't know if I'm in the twilight zone or what. I don't know what the fuck just happened.

"Poor thing, she's star struck," the tiny blonde woman says to the man who seems hell bent on destroying me and everything I care most about.

They leave the room and I sag into a chair, my phone already in my hand.

CHAPTER TWENTY-TWO

Brody

I dial Ethan's number and wait for him to answer.

He should be out of his first class by now and on his way to his second.

"Hey, Brody, what's up?" he answers.

"I'm just checking in," I say as I pace to the front window and pull back the curtain to see if Morgan has magically appeared out of thin air.

"What's going on?" he asks.

I can hear the chatter of the other students in the background, talking and yelling in the hallways.

"I don't want you to stress, but there's been a development in what's happening with your mum, and I just told her I'd give you a call and make sure you were all good."

"I'm sweet. Is Mum okay?"

"She's good, bud, she's real good, just being precautious," I ramble.

"Alright," he replies warily, like he doesn't believe me. I don't blame him. Hell, even I don't believe me.

"Look, I'll level with you, kid, some dodgy shit is going on, so if you hear anything that you don't think is right, let me know, and if you see any white sports cars hanging around, let me know about that too," I say as I run my hand through my shaggy hair.

"A white sports car?" he asks loudly over the chatter.

"Yeah, your mum thinks she might have been followed by one a few times."

I'm met with silence.

"Ethan?" I question.

"Dad drives a white sports car," he replies, and his voice sounds haunted.

"*What*?" I demand, even though I heard him loud and clear.

"Dad," he repeats. "His brand-new Mustang, it's white."

Motherfucker.

I take a deep breath through my nose.

"Where is he staying?"

"Ashbrooke Hotel," he replies without thinking twice.

I nod. That's not far from here.

"I bet it's just a coincidence," I say through clenched teeth, even though I'm sure it's not.

Ethan huffs out a laugh. "Yeah, like it was 'just a coincidence' that he came to visit right after he found out Mum had a boyfriend... and how he finally watched me play a game of basketball after he found out *you* were the coach."

"He's never watched you play?" I question.

"Nope. Never."

That breaks my fucking heart.

My throat feels thick with emotion. I try to swallow it down.

"That's his loss, Eth, okay? You're a good player and an even better kid, and the fact that he can't see that doesn't make it any less true, alright?"

He's silent.

"Alright?" I demand.

"*Yeah*... alright."

"I gotta go, alright, bud? Look after yourself and me or your mum will pick you up after school, okay? Don't go anywhere without us."

"Thanks, Brody. Mum is lucky to have you. So am I."

I'm about to tell him that I'm the lucky one, not only to have her in my life, but him too, but he's hung up.

I rake my hands over my face in frustration.

My finger hovers over the keypad, I'm about to call the police, but think twice.

The police are just going to tell me that I don't have any evidence and they'll look into it.

Looking into it isn't going to cut it.

I think this is something that might be better handled in-house.

My phone rings in my hand and I'm half expecting it to be Ethan calling to say there's something he's forgotten to tell me, when I see Morgan's name flashing across the screen.

My heart drops and I hurriedly answer. She should be in the middle of the open house, not calling me.

"Baby," I breathe, "we need to talk."

"It's Chad," she whispers, "I think it was him the whole time."

I don't know how she's figured it out, but she knows, and that's the main thing.

"I think so too, are you okay?"

"No," she replies, "he's here."

***

"Where the fuck is he?" I hiss.

"They left ten minutes ago," she whispers, her voice shaky.

I let her off the phone so I could drive and she could fill in Jerome about who he had just been dealing with.

Chad *fucking* Jenson.

The god damn psycho pretended not to know who Morgan was, even as he hurried his *wife* from the house.

At least the prick had the good sense to get out of there smartly.

If he were really smart, he'd have left town by now. Thing is, I bet he's not that smart. In fact, I'm counting on it.

I U-turn and head back downtown towards the hotel that Ethan told me Chad was staying at.

"What are you going to do, slick?" she asks quietly.

"I'm not sure yet," I answer honestly, I feel like hitting him with my car, but that isn't going to help anything or anyone.

"Get Jerome to take you home, wait for me there," I instruct her.

"Brody—"

"It's fine, baby, trust me."

"I do. I love you," she says.

"And I love you too."

I hang up the phone and toss it on the seat.

This is ending now, and not just this bullshit stalking business, not just scaring my woman and hurting her son, but the whole fucking thing.

This sixteen-year saga has gone on long enough.

Chad Jenson is nothing but a cancer in their lives and he's going to learn that I don't care how much he's worth, I'm going to make him wish he never set foot in this town.

I come to a screeching stop outside the hotel and jump out, slamming my door behind me.

I jog into the lobby and scan the area, but there's no sign of him.

I should have got here before they did, just.

I stroll around the area and pick a seat with a direct view of the doors.

If Chad can pretend *not* to know Morgan, then he can pretend that he's happy to see me too.

It doesn't take long before I see him, the small blonde woman attached to him with their linked arms.

I actually feel sorry for her; she probably has no idea what a complete psychopath her husband is.

I jump to my feet and stride to intercept them before they can get into the elevator.

"Chad!" I call loudly, turning his head. "Took you long enough to get back."

The look on his face is one of pure shock.

"And this must be Penny." I reach for her hand and clasp it in mine. "You're even prettier than he said you were."

Penny giggles and glances up at her husband, who is still standing there, shell shocked.

"I'm sorry, but who are you?" she questions.

"Sorry, forgive my rudeness, I'm Brody, an old friend of Chad's."

"Oh *Brody*, hi, yes Chad told me *all* about you."

I refrain from chuckling. She's at least got enough manners to lie.

"How was the house?" I ask as though he's told me their plans, "you interested in buying it?"

Once again, it's Penny who answers, "Oh no, I don't think so... it was a beautiful home, but Chad was just humouring me. He comes down about once a year for business, and since I was on maternity leave this time, I insisted I come with him. It's so beautiful here, I thought we could move, but I don't think it's going to happen." She pouts.

"That's a shame," I reply.

She nods in agreement as I turn my attention to her piece-of-shit husband.

"What about you, man, you see anything you liked while you were there?"

Chad snaps out of it then, blinking hard.

"It was a surprising property," he replies.

"Let's go for that beer, yeah? Catch up. You want to come, Penny?"

"Oh I—"

"Penny was just going up for a rest, it's been a long morning for her, you know with the baby and everything," he interrupts as he gestures to her rounded belly, a not-so-subtle gesture that his wife is in a fragile state.

It's a fair call. This isn't on her and I don't need a premature labour on my conscience anyway.

"Well it was so good to meet you, finally," I tell her, laying it on thick. "I might see you next time?"

Chad kisses the top of her head and pushes the button for the lift for her.

The doors slide open and he shoves his bewildered-looking wife inside. "I'll be up soon," he tells her and then she's gone.

The minute the doors close, I swing, hitting him clean across the jaw.

"Fuck," he grunts, as he hunches over, wiping at the blood coming from his mouth.

I hear gasps all around us, but I don't care that we're in the lobby of one of the most expensive hotels in town.

This is happening *now*.

If he wanted privacy, he shouldn't have come after my girl. He should have talked to me man to man. He shouldn't have been a crazy fucker.

He stands back up, glaring at me.

"Just let me—"

I hit him again, this time in his gut. I hear his breath leave him with a whoosh.

He doubles over, his knees sinking to the ground.

"I didn't know she would be there," he chokes out.

"But you knew everywhere else she'd be, didn't you? You fucking *stalker*."

He looks up at me, his eyes wide. Stupid fucking pretty boy isn't as smart as he thinks he is. That reaction is all the confirmation I need.

"What did you think would happen, huh? You'd scare her and it'd break us up? Or are you a total sick fuck and you really did want to hurt her?"

"I'd never lay a finger on her," he says, and honestly, it's the only thing to come out of his mouth that I do believe.

My chest is heaving with exertion, not from hitting him, but from resisting the urge to hit him again.

He gets to his feet slowly, wiping again at the blood in his mouth.

"She's too good for you," he spits.

I laugh darkly. "No fucking shit. She's too good for *every-one*, the woman is an angel."

He opens his mouth to speak, but I cut him off. I didn't come here to hear him out, or to justify my relationship, I came here to tell him exactly how it's going to be from now on.

"This shit stops *now*. You don't contact her; you don't come near her. You certainly don't follow her in your fancy fucking car."

An arrogant smirk twitches at his bloody lip, like he's pleased with himself.

"If I see you anywhere near Morgan again, I won't just tell your pretty little wife what a low life you are, I'll go to the police too – I'll ruin your fucking career in a heartbeat."

His smirk slips. He can see I'm not talking shit. I mean it.

"The only reason I'm not doing that already is because she's pregnant." I point at the lift his wife disappeared into. "I've seen what you've done to Ethan, and it's not that kid's fault you're a complete prick." I sneer.

His eyes dip to the floor and then back up to my face. He knows I've got him beat.

He nods once.

"And as far as Ethan goes, if you want to see him, you'll do it through me, and if you don't start treating him with some respect, then you're gone, end of. Frankly, I'd cut you off from seeing him ever again right here and now, but I haven't discussed it with Ethan yet so that's not my call to make. If he doesn't want to see you, then you don't come back. Understood?"

He nods again.

"Now get the fuck out of my sight."

He straightens his shoulders, trying to salvage the tiny bit of dignity he's got left and walks towards the lift.

"Oh and, Chad?" I call after him.

He turns to face me, and I can't help it. I hit him once more.

"Fuck you," I hiss before I walk away.

EPILOGUE

Brody

"And now I'm handing over to Ethan Bradley, our most valuable player for the season, who wants to say a few quick words," Anthony, my assistant coach announces as he hands off the microphone to Ethan.

Ethan takes the mic, a cocky smirk on his face as his eyes find mine in the crowd.

I don't know why, but I feel like I'm about to be thrown under the bus, big time.

"Hey everyone," he says, "I couldn't let the speeches finish without thanking the man who did so much for us this season, he coached us to the championship final and was right there with us when we became national champions."

A chorus of cheers breaks out from the players around the room. "Go cubs!" and "whoo, whoo, whoo!" fills the air.

I grin. Adam's nickname stuck.

Morgan's hand squeezes my knee from her spot on the chair next to me.

She looks so happy and carefree.

She's got no reason not to be now.

Chad is long gone, the creep from the bar is serving jail time, and she's safe.

Ethan told his dad that he wanted nothing to do with him once it was confirmed that it was Chad who had been trying to scare Morgan.

I'm confident he won't be back any time soon.

"Let's get him up here." Ethan points at me.

"Yeah, Coach!"

"C'mon, Coach!"

"You're the man, Coach Owens!"

Cheers surround me as I get to my feet, shaking my head in amusement.

Ethan grins wider, and I just know he's got something up his sleeve.

I make my way to the stage and stand next to him, my arms crossed against my chest.

"You look worried, Coach." He chuckles.

"That's because I *am* worried."

Laughter floats through the room.

He turns back to the crowd, he's really warming up to this public speaking now, he looks in his element. I might have to make him captain next year.

Morgan was right – I got offered a senior coaching position at the end of the season.

I don't think anyone was more surprised than me when I turned it down. I'm not ready to leave the kids yet. Maybe one day, but not right now.

"So, everyone already knows that Coach is dating my mum, right?"

I groan.

The boys all whoop and holler. I think the mums cheer even louder.

Morgan covers her face with her hands.

"So, I figure that means I owe him some type of public humiliation, right?"

I hear Hunter yelling out, 'Yeah, man!', and most of the other boys joining in too.

"I can't take all the credit for this," Ethan says, barely containing his laughter, "It was a *team effort*."

He points at the screen behind us and I turn.

"What in the fuck..."

They're projecting a huge image on the screen, it's a guy in his underwear, with my face badly photoshopped onto the body. Underneath are the words 'Mr. September'.

"Mr. September, ladies and gentlemen," Ethan manages to say between fits of laugher.

Everyone in the room is laughing and clapping.

"I don't get it," I deadpan, looking at him to explain what the hell is going on.

Ethan laughs harder. "You're the new Mr. September – the charming coach."

The room fills with chatter as everyone laughs and jokes.

"I'm the *what*?" I demand.

Ethan sits the mic on the table and smirks at me again.

"This lady came in the other night when we were training – that night you left early, looking for someone to model for this calendar she's doing, so we volunteered you. Better get in the gym coach, you're getting your kit off."

"You *didn't*." I gape at him.

He starts laughing all over again.

Adam comes up on stage, grinning widely, wiping tears from his eyes.

"You," I point at him, "you were in on this, weren't you?"

"You shacked up with the kid's mum, you owe him, man." He chuckles.

"Can't leave you in charge for five minutes," I grumble.

He raises his hands and shrugs. "Just embrace it."

I look helplessly at Ethan. "There's no getting out of this, is there?"

He shakes his head victoriously. "Since you've always got your shirt off at home, I figured you'd be in your element."

I reach out to clip him around the ears, but he ducks, grinning. I can't help but laugh.

Fuck my life.

"You guys suck."

"But you love us." Adam grins.

I run my hand through my hair and search through the masses of people for Morgan.

She's sitting next to Olivia and they're whispering and grinning like they knew this was going to happen all along.

As cunning as they are, I love how close they've become.

"Your mum knew about this too?" I ask Ethan, my eyes never leaving my woman.

"No comment," he replies.

"You're really gonna make me do this?"

He nods eagerly. "You'll be a chicken shit if you don't." He chuckles.

My mind spins and I turn to him. "I'll make you a deal."

He crosses his arms and narrows his eyes at me. "What kind of deal?"

I beckon him forward and he leans in so I can whisper my offer in his ear.

He pulls back, looking at me with a surprised expression. "Really?" he asks.

I nod. "If that's okay with you?"

His eyes glaze over, but he blinks quickly, clears his throat and nods. "It's more than okay with me."

I grab his shoulder and pull him in for a hug.

He's still for a minute before he hugs me back, gripping me tightly.

He pulls away, clears his throat again, claps me on the shoulder and heads off towards his buddies.

I get the feeling that's the first time he's been hugged by a man who really cares about him.

I weave back through the crowd, getting teased and joked with the whole way until I reach Morgan, who's sitting there looking thoroughly amused.

"You're in trouble, Morgs."

She bites down on her lip. "Maybe I like trouble, slick."

I crouch down in front of her, so our faces are level. "You're going to have to make this up to me."

"You *know* I'm up for that." She grins devilishly.

My mind gets distracted and I have to shake my head to clear my thoughts before I sneak her out of here for some one-on-one practice in the changing sheds.

"Good, because me and Ethan have made a deal."

"More basketball tickets?" she asks, her brow raised.

I shake my head.

She gives me a 'well tell me' look and I chuckle.

"Not quite. It's more of a geographical deal..."

She frowns in confusion.

"Move in with me?" I ask.

Her brows shoot up in surprise. "*That's* the deal you made with Ethan?"

I shrug.

It's not the only question I asked him, but it's the only one I want to share now. I need to get a ring before I even think about asking her the other one.

"And he wants to?"

"I mean, I think he just wants to see me embarrass myself in this photoshoot, but yeah, he told me we had a deal."

"And what if I said no?"

"Then I guess Ethan will have to move in without you." I chuckle.

I might be playing it cool, but my heart is going crazy in my chest. I want her to say yes.

We spend nearly every night together anyway – she's it for me. I just want to get on with our lives together.

"You really don't mind the idea of living with a teenage boy?"

I scoff at her. "I *was* a teenage boy once. They're just misunderstood."

She giggles. "And you won't complain when he's always eating all the food?"

"I'll get him his own fridge."

She looks right into my eyes. "You really want to be 'Brody from tonight', every night?"

I chuckle at the reference to our first text exchange. "I really do."

She smiles softly. "Alright, slick... we'll move in."

I claim her lips with mine and she giggles softly against me.

"I love you," I murmur.

"I love you too." She sighs.

OTHER TITLES

Love like Yours Series
Rushed – Book 1
Pierced – Book 2
Hunted – Book 3
Chased – Book 4

Rock Games Novels
Paper, Scissors, Rock: Vol. 1
Hide and Seek: Vol. 2

My Heart Duet
My Heart Needs
My Heart Wants

Calendar Boys Novels
Mr. January
Mr. February
Mr. March
Mr. April
Mr. May
Mr. June
Mr. July
Mr. August
Mr. September

ACKNOWLEDGEMENTS

The songs that inspired this book, *Halo* – Jasmine Thompson, *Peer Pressure* – James Bay and Julia Michaels and *In Love Again* – Colbie Caillat.

We're getting towards the end of the series now, and I'm still having so much fun with the boys and their leading ladies – if you're still with me, thanks so much! I really appreciate you reading and loving my characters as much as I do.

To my usual support crew, thank so much, as always... you know who you are!

Roll on October!

ABOUT THE AUTHOR

NICOLE S. GOODIN is a romance author and mother of two from Taranaki in the North Island of New Zealand.

In mid-2015, she started to write about a group of characters who wouldn't get out of her head. Her first book, Rushed, was published in mid-2016.

Nicole enjoys long walks on the beach, pillow fights and braiding her friends' hair. She dislikes clichés, talking about herself in the third person, and people who don't understand her sense of humour.

Please feel free to contact her either via her website, email, Instagram, Twitter or on her Facebook page, she would love to hear your feedback. If you're feeling really game, you can even sign up for her newsletter.

Visit www.nicolegoodinauthor.com for more information.

UPCOMING TITLES

Calendar Boys Novels

Mr. October
Mr. November
Mr. December